A MAN POSSESSED

Life seems idyllic for interior designers Rosalind and James Camarthey, living in the smart London flat they designed together as a showpiece for their combined talents. Then, soon after Rosalind turns down a lucrative job to stay with James, things begin to go badly wrong. Her fairytale marriage seems to crumble about her ears. James announces his intention of moving to Paris, and Rosalind has new fears to contend with in the shape of smart, glamorous Lisa, the secretary who seems to share more of James's life than Rosalind nowadays. The only person who seems to understand is the enigmatic Troy Ballard, who buys a derelict property in the Cotswolds and asks Rosalind to turn it into a home...

A MAN POSSESSED

Donna Baker

CHIVERS PRESS
BATH

First published 1996
by
Severn House Publishers
This Large Print edition published by
Chivers Press
by arrangement with
Severn House Publishers
1997

ISBN 0 7451 5461 1

British Library Cataloguing in Publication Data available

Photoset, printed and bound in Great Britain by
REDWOOD BOOKS, Trowbridge, Wiltshire

CHAPTER ONE

Rosalind drove into the underground car park and swung into the reserved space. She switched off the engine and sat for a moment, relaxing before turning to heave out the cumbersome books of samples. Then, clutching them to her new designer suit, she scrambled out, locked the door and made for the lift which would carry her up to the tenth floor of the block of flats. As she was whisked up through the tall, quiet building, she wondered if James were home yet.

It was unusual for them not to be coming home together, and she could have done with his help this evening. But he had been out to visit a new client and Rosalind was looking forward to hearing about it over their meal. One of her favourite ways of spending an evening with her husband was to discuss a new job with him. It was always different and always exciting working as an interior decorator, whether it was in a mansion in the country or a tiny mews flat in Town. She wondered what it was going to be this time.

Meanwhile, she had her own project to talk over with him. And as the lift stopped at their floor, she gave the sample books an approving pat. James was going to really like these, she knew it.

But when she walked into the flat, confidently expecting him to be waiting for her with a drink ready to be poured, it was still in darkness.

Rosalind frowned. James ought to be home by now. He knew what time she got back, and he knew that she'd prepared a casserole for their meal this evening—she could smell it now, rich and warm from the slow cooker she had set that morning. Where was he?

Half irritated, half concerned, she walked over to the big picture window and stared out at the lights of London. They spread out as far as she could see, a sparkling carpet of colour that more than made up for the blackness of the sky. In the country, where Rosalind had grown up with her mother, the aspect was reversed—a glittering firmament of needle-point stars that hung over the darkness of the unlit fields and moors like a great, upturned bowl. You never really saw the stars in London, and even the moon was dulled by comparison with the brightness of the city lights.

Suddenly impatient, she pulled the cord that swung the curtains across the window, and went to turn on the lamps, filling the cool, white room with soft light. Where *was* James?

At that moment, she heard his key in the door. Eagerly, she turned, smoothing her long, silky hair down with fingers that suddenly shook. Really, she thought, it was ridiculous to feel like this—like an excited young girl, out on her first date. She'd been married to James for three years, for heaven's sake! Yet he still had this power to make her knees tremble and her heart quicken, whenever they'd been apart from even a few hours. No wonder she never wanted to be away from him!

All the same, she was still slightly annoyed that he hadn't been here when she came home, and when he came through the tiny hall and into the big, white lounge, she stood waiting for him rather than run into his arms as she would normally have done.

'Ros? I'm home,' James called from the hall, and then came into the room like a sudden gale. How was it he always seemed to bring this impression of having strode straight in from a grouse moor rather than a London street? It certainly wasn't his clothes—James dressed impeccably always, even if slightly unconventionally. His suits were sharp, his shirts the latest design, his dark hair always cut in the most up-to-date style, his shoes gleaming. But there was always something just a little individual about his style, something no other man would think of. A brilliant paisley handkerchief in his breast pocket, perhaps, or a fun watch rather than the gold Rolex Rosalind had given him when they married. Some little touch that drew the eye and spoke of an individuality that would shake off convention without a moment's regret if that

3

was what James decided.

Their clients liked this. That was why they asked for him, time and time again. That little hint of individuality that added spark to the aura of prosperous reliability that surrounded him. And that air of having come in from some really tough, outdoor job. Like felling trees, or breaking in difficult horses. An air that quelled any suggestion of preciousness and made the fact of James's virile masculinity absolutely without question.

Rosalind felt her heart thump, as it always did. She waited for him to sweep across the room like a storm and kiss her. She felt her tongue flick involuntarily round her lips, wetting them. But James did not cross the room. He stood just inside the door, staring at her, and she felt a twinge of something very like fear at the expression in his dark, narrowed eyes. 'James?' she said uncertainly, taking a step forward and then hesitating. *Fear?* Could she really be feeling afraid of James, of her husband? Surely not! And yet ... 'James ... what is it, darling?'

'You tell me,' he said, almost on a growl. 'You just tell me, Rosalind.'

Rosalind. He almost never called her that. Only when he was angry with her, and they rarely quarrelled. She felt a frown gather on her smooth forehead and cast a quick glance sideways into the gold-framed mirror that hung on the wall. Was something wrong with her appearance?

No—she looked the same as usual. Pale, silky hair sweeping like a silvery waterfall below her shoulders. Smooth, oval face, slightly slanted dark blue eyes, full, rose-pink lips ... nothing different there. She looked back at James, shook her head and moved forward again, hands held out, palms upwards. 'But I've nothing to tell you, darling. Nothing's happened since lunchtime. I've been thinking over the decor for the master bedroom for Cyndy Burnett's flat—look, I brought some samples home.' She bent to the coffee table where she had dropped the sample books. 'I found these—a new line. I think she'll love them. This bright pink, it's just her colour, and the toning mauves moving into soft blue—I can just see her in these. What do you think?'

She was talking rapidly, uncomfortable at first but gaining confidence as she moved into the world they shared and understood. But as she continued, describing the new idea she'd had for hanging the curtains, the matching bed canopy and the carpet, she began to falter and feel her discomfort return. James wasn't reacting at all. He was just standing there, silent, unresponsive. What was wrong?

She floundered to a halt and straightened up, looking at him. 'James, what *is* the matter? What's happened? You'd better tell me.'

He moved at last, flinging himself on to one of the creamy-white sofas. They'd designed

5

this room together, as they had shared in the decoration of all the flat, turning it from a dark vault into this space of light and brightness. Only a few spots of colour sparked into life: a scarlet cushion here, a piece of jade there, a shimmering golden frame on the wall, around a gleaming mirror or modern print; each of them picking up one of the colours from the curtains that were a brilliant shout across the window wall. Rosalind loved it.

But now, her pleasure in the room was dimmed. She stared down at her husband and then dropped to her knees on the shaggy white rug beside him. Something was terribly wrong. James was angry with her. And she couldn't even begin to think why. 'James...'

He turned his head, looked into her eyes. His voice, normally so deep and tender, was rough—almost harsh. 'I ran into Brent Woodford on my way home this evening. We went for a drink together.'

'Oh. So that's why you weren't home when I got here. I wondered where you were. I was worried, James.'

He sighed. 'Yes, I rather thought you might be.' But he didn't apologise, she noticed. 'Rosalind, did you hear what I said? I ran into Brent Woodford. *Brent Woodford*. We had a drink together.'

'Yes, I heard—' Suddenly, she caught his implication. 'Oh.'

'Yes. "Oh."' His gaze was brooding. 'You

6

don't need me to tell you what we talked about, Ros.'

At least he was calling her Ros again. She shrugged, as if it couldn't matter less. 'Well, yes, I suppose he told you about the job. So what? It's not important, is it?'

'*Not important?* You get offered one of the best jobs going in the interior design business and you shrug it off and say it's *not important*? Of *course* it's important, Ros. And what's even more important is that you didn't even bother to mention it to me.'

'Why should I? I turned it down. End of story.'

'No,' he said, and his voice was taut with an anger she realised he hadn't even begun to express. 'No, it is *not* the end of the story. It's just the beginning. I want to know what in hell you think you're playing at, Ros. And just what our marriage means to you. So why don't we have a cosy evening discussing just that?'

Rosalind stared at him. Her heart was beating fast. James had never spoken to her like this before, and she felt frightened and upset. And yet, hard on the heels of those feelings, she felt anger. How *dare* he speak to her in this way? Wasn't it *her* business what job she took or didn't take? Wasn't it her life?

'All right,' she said tensely. 'As it happens, I was going to suggest we look at these samples I took the trouble to lug home for you to see, but you're obviously not interested. I was also going to ask you all about the new job you went to see this afternoon, but it seems you don't want to share that with me either. So yes, let's discuss why I shouldn't make up my own mind on how I spend my working day, and what possible effect that could have on our marriage. Do you want to eat first, or later? Shall we make an appointment for it or plunge straight into a row?'

James gave her a glance of pure exasperation. 'Why should everything have to turn into a row? I just suggested we spend some time discussing our marriage. Am I suppose to put samples of somebody else's carpets and curtains before that? For God's sake, I thought that was what most normal women *wanted* to do? I thought it was all they were interested in—spending hours chewing over this and that detail of their personal relationships. I thought you'd be *pleased* that I was more interested in us than in a few cushion covers.'

Rosalind bit her lip. 'You don't have to put me in the wrong—'

'*I'm* not putting you anywhere. You're exactly where you put yourself.' He shrugged. 'If that happens to be in the wrong, and even you can see that—'

'James!' Rosalind stared at him. 'James, what are we quarrelling about? I've lost my place in this discussion. Look, all I did was have lunch with Brent and he offered me a job and I turned it down. What's so terrible about

8

that?'

'I didn't say anything was terrible,' he said. 'All I said was we should have discussed it. I would have encouraged you to accept. It would have been a good move for you. Now the chance has gone.'

'But I didn't *want* it!' she cried. 'There wouldn't have been any point in a discussion. I wouldn't have taken the job anyway. Because I don't want to move away from Lords & Ladies. I don't want to move away from *you.*'

There was a long silence. Then James looked directly into her eyes. She tried in vain to analyse his expression and couldn't. Again, she felt a tremor of fear. She had always known what James was thinking before...

His eyes were the darkest brown she had ever seen, and now looked almost black, the pupils so wide that there was no more than a rim of mahogany. For a moment, he held her gaze and then he shook his head and reached out for her hands.

'Ros, don't let's quarrel over this. I came home in a bit of a mood, I admit, but I don't want it to come between us. I just want to know why you refused that job—'

'Because I didn't want it, that's why. Because I'm happy where I am. Is that so hard to understand?' She tightened her fingers in his. 'James, surely you realise what it would have meant. We work together, you and I. And I want it to stay that way. I didn't want to go to

9

some other firm and leave you.' She gazed at him appealingly. 'Can't you understand that?'

James shook his head. 'No, I can't. You've always called yourself a career girl, Ros. You've prided yourself on your ability, your independence. You made it quite clear that your job, your *career*, mean a lot to you. So why turn down a chance like Brent was offering you? It doesn't make sense.'

'But I've told you. I turned it down for *you*. Yes, my career does mean a a lot to me—but not more than being with you. That's what means most.'

'Are you sure?' he asked. 'Are you sure you're not just afraid to strike out alone? Maybe you're scared of failing. And if you'd talked to me, I could have reassured you, helped you—'

Rosalind snatched her hands away. 'How can you say that? Of course I'm not scared of failing—I know I'm good at my job, I could have held down the job Brent offered me too. It's nothing to do with that!' Her breath was coming quickly and she could feel the heat in her cheeks. 'James, just what is this? Do you *want* me to move on, is that it? Don't you want me working with you?' Fear struck her like a blow, and her voice shook as she whispered, 'James, don't you love me any more?'

'Of course I love you—'

'Then why are you so keen for me to leave Lords & Ladies? Maybe there's some other reason.' She stared at him, trying to read the expression in his eyes, but all at once he was a stranger. 'Maybe it's that glamorous new secretary you've got—Lisa. Maybe you want me out of the way so that you and she—'

'*Rosalind!*' His voice was like a whip. 'Stop it! You don't know what you're saying—of course there's nothing between me and Lisa. She's just a very efficient, very good secretary, nothing more, and you know it. You're getting all this out of proportion—'

'Am I? Am I, James? Then why are you so keen for me to leave Lords & Ladies? *Why don't you want me working near you any more?*'

James sighed. He let go of her hands and took her face between his palms. 'Ros, calm down and listen. You know perfectly well that I love you and I love working with you. But we agreed when we got married that we would both keep our careers, at least until we decided to start a family. That didn't mean we had to stay still for the rest of our lives. It meant we would work to the best of our ability, fulfilling whatever potential we each had. Now you've had a chance to expand, fly a bit higher. It's because I love you that I want you to take the opportunity—not because I want to get rid of you. Surely you can see that?'

Rosalind was silent for a moment. Then she said, slowly, 'Yes, I can see that. But what you can't seem to see is that I'm happy with my career as it is. I like what I do and I like it best of

11

all because we're near each other. I don't want to fly, to expand. If we could do it together—that would be different. But Brent wasn't offering *us* a job—he was offering it to me. And I just wasn't interested on that basis.'

She stopped and looked at him. Putting her feelings into words suddenly brought home their vital importance to her. James *must* understand it. It was as if their whole life together depended upon his understanding now. If he couldn't see that she wanted to spend all her time with him, at work as well as at home, that she wanted—needed—to share every possible moment with him ... if he couldn't see that, what use was their marriage? She had a sudden, frightening vision of an empty shell, and her heart recoiled.

James's expression was unreadable. His eyes were veiled, as if a curtain had come down over his thoughts. He took his hands from her face and stroked her fingers gently, and when he spoke, his voice was soft, warm, the voice of the tender, loving James she knew so well. But the words were at odds with his tone: 'Ros, darling, of course I understand that. But what worries me is that you didn't give me the chance to talk it over with you. You didn't give *us* the chance. You just went ahead and said no without even mentioning it to me, and—'

'But there was no *point* in mentioning it!' she cried. 'I knew I didn't want to take it. I'd forgotten all about it by the time I saw you again, anyway—it was that day you went down to Kent to see the final touches on Holt Manor. Brent rang me and invited me to lunch, and over dessert he told me about the job and asked if I'd like it. Naturally, I said no at once and—'

'*Naturally*?' James broke in. 'Ros, what was "natural" about that? Brent must have thought you were crazy. Didn't he ask you to think it over?'

'Yes, he did, but I didn't need to. I told him I wouldn't change my mind, and I told him why.'

James stared at her. He let go of one of her hands and ran his fingers through his dark hair. 'You told him why? You told him you wouldn't take this *fabulous* job he was offering you because you wanted to go on working with me?'

'Yes, I did.' Ros lifted her chin slightly and met his eyes. 'And what's so wrong with that? I like working with you. I don't want to do anything else. And the job I've got is good—I don't need Brent Woodford's glamour. Why should I let him rule my life?'

James shook his head. 'Ros, we're getting off the point. What concerns me is not that you turned down the job—that's OK, if it's what you want. You know all I want is for you to be happy, either climbing the ladder or staying on whatever rung you find most comfortable. What worries me is that you did this without even thinking of discussing it with me—'

13

'But I keep telling you—there was nothing to discuss—'

'*There was!*' He wrenched his fingers away from hers and jumped to his feet, striding about the room like a caged panther. By the window, he turned and stared at her, and she flinched away from the expression in his eyes. 'Ros, we're married, right? So when a big decision comes up, we make it *together*. And you may think this was no big deal, it was your business to decide; it's your life, and you may be right. I'm sure that if we had discussed it we'd have come to the same conclusion, if that's what you wanted. I'm not going to push you to do things you don't want to do. But the point is that we ought to *share* these things. We ought to talk them over together.'

His glance fell on the books of fabric samples that Rosalind had brought home. 'We spend hours talking about other people's furnishings,' he said bitterly, 'and almost none talking about ourselves and our own life. And that's what bothers me.'

'But other people's furnishings *are* our life,' Rosalind said blankly, and fell silent at the look in James's eyes.

'I know. And does that seem to you to be what marriage is all about?'

There was a long silence. James came slowly away from the window and dropped into a chair. He stared at the big metal sculpture that stood where a fireplace might once have been.

14

Ros noticed the tired lines on his face and felt a momentary pang. But his words were still hammering in her brain.

Unable to sit still any longer, she rose to her feet. 'You're making a big issue out of something that doesn't really matter at all,' she said coldly. 'If you'd not met Brent Woodford tonight, you'd never have known about this. He'd have forgotten about it in another week or so. As for making big decisions together, of course we do. I just didn't consider this a big decision, that's all.' She stopped. He was still turned away from her, his face shuttered.

On a sudden impulse, she went to him and dropped on her knees beside him. 'James, don't let's make a quarrel out of this,' she begged. 'It's a silly little thing. You know how much I value our marriage. It's everything—*you're* everything—to me. That's why I want to stay with you, working together. I love being at Lords & Ladies with you. I love knowing that we're in the same building most of the time, that I only have to walk down a corridor to be with you, that we can discuss our work together. I love working on the same houses with you.

'Look—' She turned and pulled the sample books towards her, '—just look at these. I've been dying to show them to you ever since I found them. A whole new range—a really exciting young designer. I've been looking forward all day to showing them to you. Let's

15

forget all this, shall we, and have a meal and then go through them. I know you're going to like them just as much as I do.'

James turned his head at last. He looked into her eyes. He reached out a hand and laid it on her shoulder, and shook his head slightly. Then, at last, he smiled. It wasn't his usual loving smile. But it was a start, and Ros sat back on her heels, feeling the relief flood through her.

'All right, Ros. Let's do that. I'll set the table while you get the casserole served up. And then we'll look at these new designs you've found.'

Smiling with relief, Rosalind scrambled to her feet and made for the kitchen. 'It'll be five minutes. And let's open a bottle of wine as well, shall we?' She had an obscure feeling there was something to celebrate. For a few moments, it had seemed as if her whole world were rocking on its axis, about to topple over and fall into a deep, dark abyss. Now, everything was all right again. 'We'll use the best crystal glasses,' she called as she put two potatoes into the microwave oven and plugged in the platewarmer. And why not? Wasn't every night she spent with James a celebration? Wasn't their whole life together a celebration of their love?

Of course she would never leave him to go and work for another—a rival—firm.

*　　*　　*

16

'... so you'll both come down at the weekend?' Sheila Mitchell's voice was warm with pleasure. 'That's lovely, darling. I'll buy a fatted calf especially. It seems ages since I last saw you, we'll have a lot to catch up on. I'm longing to hear all about your latest projects.'

Rosalind felt a spurt of irritation. How was it that her mother always seemed to manage to make her feel guilty, even when she was expressing pleasure? Was it her imagination, or was there really a hidden reproach in those words? *Buy a fatted calf... ages since I last saw you ... a lot to catch up on?* She couldn't say anything, of course—Sheila would simply stare and laugh and tell her she was being over-sensitive.

Well, maybe she was. Maybe it was her own guilty conscience picking up on these things. After all, she didn't see all that much of her mother, did she? It was two months now since she and James had been down to the Cotswolds to visit her. And her weekly phone calls had been rather short lately. She couldn't blame Sheila for feeling a little lonely and left out.

'We'll come on Friday evening,' she promised, hoping that James wouldn't mind the change of plan. 'And stay till Sunday teatime.' That meant not getting back to the flat until the middle of the evening—too late to do anything but just potter about for an hour or two before going to bed. But if it satisfied her

17

mother . . . And they needn't go again for a few weeks. Not until Christmas, in fact.

She sighed. They'd hoped to spend Christmas with James's family this year but now, listening to Sheila's delighted exclamations, she wondered whether they really would. How could she enjoy the big, family celebrations, knowing that her mother was on her own? Already, she could feel the tug of guilt, and—as always—it was quickly followed by anger that she could still be so affected by it. She was independent, wasn't she? And had been for years.

'All right,' she said when Sheila stopped talking about her plans for the weekend. 'We'll see you soon after seven. Yes, I'll ring if it's going to be any later. Yes, we'll take care, you know James is a good driver. Yes, I'll bring the pictures of Holt Manor and the plans for Cyndy Burnett's flat. You'll like the new fabrics I've found.'

At least they'd have plenty to talk about. Sheila was as interested in Rosalind's job as an interior decorator as she was in her own little antiques business in the little Cotswold town. In fact, she'd always been totally encouraging in Rosalind's choice of career. It was what she'd always longed to do herself.

So why, when Rosalind put down the phone, did she feel this sense of oppression? As if she were still struggling to free herself of some tie?

She came slowly out of the bedroom and

18

walked across to the big window, staring absently over the glittering, rain-wet rooftops of London.

James, sitting on the white couch, lowered his newspaper. 'Been talking to your mother? How is she?'

'Oh, just the same as usual. I said we'd go down on Friday instead of waiting till Saturday morning. You don't mind, do you?'

'Not if you don't.' But there was a touch of restraint in his voice and Rosalind turned to look at him.

'You do mind.'

'I don't. Not at all. But I've a feeling that you do.' He gave her a quizzical glance. 'Am I right?'

Rosalind sighed and came to sit beside him. He laid his arm around her shoulder and she rested her head against his chest. He was warm and comforting, and she breathed in the male scent of him and thought how lucky she was. And how lonely her mother must have been since her husband, John Mitchell, had died all those years ago. 'Why does she always make me feel so guilty, James? She's always encouraged me so much—to train in art and design, to go in for interior decorating, to live in London. Yet when I talk to her, I get the feeling she has me in chains and I resent it. And then I feel guilty for resenting it! Yet all she wants is to see me occasionally, and keep in touch, and be a part of my life still. And it's not

19

so much to ask—I'm all she's got.'

'I know. And it makes it very difficult for you.' He hesitated and then, seeming to choose his words with care, said, 'Just how much do you feel she has a right to ask of you, Ros?'

Rosalind lifted her head, looking at him with astonishment. 'Why, anything any mother has a right to ask of her daughter, of course. Love and affection—gratitude, I suppose—caring. She's entitled to all of those—she's my mother. She did everything for me.'

'Of course. But does she actually have a *right* to ask those things? Or should they be given freely?'

'But I do give them freely!' Rosalind sat up straight, staring at him. 'I don't look on visiting my mother as a duty!'

'Don't you?' he asked. 'Are you sure?'

'Yes, I *am* sure!' Rosalind pushed back her hair with a nervous gesture. 'I love her—she's my mother. I just wish—' She stopped.

'You wish she didn't make you feel guilty. But that means you must think you've got something to feel guilty about. And so must she.'

Rosalind stared at him, then turned abruptly away. 'Oh, I don't know what you're talking about! You're saying some very funny things lately, James. In fact, ever since I turned down that job with Brent Woodford—' She stopped again, staring at him. 'That's it, isn't it? You're still brooding over that. And do you know

20

something? I've realised why.' Almost without realising it, she was drawing away from him. 'You're jealous because he didn't offer *you* the job. Even after I'd refused it. You think he should have come to you first. That's it, isn't it?'

James gave her an exasperated look. 'No, it's not. I haven't the least desire to work for Brent and the job he offered you wouldn't have suited me at all. But I think it would have suited you very well indeed. However, we're not talking about that now, we were talking about your mother.'

He held out his arm, inviting her to come back into its circle. 'Ros, don't let's start arguing again. We seem to be doing it so much just lately. Let's try to get back to how we used to be—happy and comfortable together.'

Rosalind looked at him. She looked at the broad, strong body which had comforted her so often, against which she could rest and relax. And which, at other times, could rouse her to such dizzy heights of passionate delight, bringing her a different sort of comfort, a haven after the wild storms of rapturous love-making.

He was right. They did seem to spend a lot of time arguing lately and often over silly, trivial things that didn't really matter at all.

Why? What was going wrong between them?

Fear suddenly invaded her body, bringing a shiver to her skin, a deep, sinking feeling to her

21

stomach. And she dropped down beside him and buried her head once more against his chest, clinging to him and seeking the comfort she needed, even though she could not understand why she needed it.

She and James had all they wanted, all they could ever need. So why did she feel this fear, this emptiness, as if it were all to be taken away from her?

Why was she so desperately afraid that she was going to lose him?

CHAPTER TWO

'So there you are!' Sheila Mitchell came quickly out of the front door as James pulled the car up in the drive. 'I was getting worried about you. This awful fog!'

'That's what made us late.' Rosalind pulled her bag from the back seat and closed the car door. 'And we're not *that* late—it isn't seven-thirty yet.'

'Seven thirty-one, actually,' her mother amended. 'Don't worry, it's all right, darling.' She turned to James, who had just climbed out of the car. 'And how are you, James?' She reached up to kiss her son-in-law. 'It's quite ridiculous but you seem taller every time I see you! Or am I shrinking in my old age?' She made a comical face. 'Come in, both of you,

22

out of the cold. Ugh—winter really is coming, isn't it? I do so hate this dismal weather.'

She led the way into the cottage, talking as she went, saying how lovely it was to see them, how kind it was of them to spare the time to come . . . And with every step, with every word, Rosalind's heart grew heavier. What *was* it that made her feel so guilty whenever she saw her mother? A guilt that brought with it, hard on its heels, the misery of resentment. Why did it have to spoil each visit, even before she was in the house?

'You've nothing to feel guilty about,' James had told her, over and over again. 'Sheila's fine. Just let her live her own life.'

'Let *her* live *her* life?' Rosalind had exclaimed. 'James, it's the other way round— she won't let me live mine.' And then she'd stopped, knowing that she could say nothing that would back up this statement. Hadn't Sheila encouraged her to go to art college, to learn design, to go for a job in London? And she'd closed her mouth, feeling even more guilty at the treachery in her own words, and even less able to understand it.

As they walked through the door, she felt James's hand on her arm and turned to look at him. He gave her a reassuring smile, as if he knew exactly what she was thinking, and she grinned back a little shamefacedly. All right, she told him silently, I know I'm over-reacting. I'll be good.

The cottage was cosy and welcoming, every corner warmed by the central heating Sheila had installed a few years ago, and from the kitchen came an appetising aroma. At Sheila's suggestion, James took their bags straight up to the bedroom they always used, and Rosalind followed her mother into the sitting room. She dropped on to the sofa and held out her hands to the log fire.

'This is nice. You know, I only realise how good a real fire is when I see yours.' She looked round the room, carefully furnished as Sheila thought a country cottage should be: the chintz covers, the flowery curtains, pretty wallpaper. Even the ornaments and pictures had been chosen to complement the cottage itself and to give the same impression of simple country life—although Rosalind was well aware that there was nothing simple or inexpensive about this room, or the rest of the cottage. Everything had taken a long time to track down and consider, and nothing had come by chance. There was no jarring note. And yet...

No, Rosalind told herself, she was just imagining that there was something missing. She was being over-sensitive again. She'd caught herself doing it several times lately— ever since Brent Woodford had offered her that job. Ever since she and James had quarrelled over it...

'Gin and tonic, darling?' Sheila was coming into the room with a tray of bottles and glasses.

24

'You must be desperate for a drink after that awful drive.'

Rosalind accepted a drink and smiled up at her mother. Sheila was looking well, she thought, the silver hair neatly cut and shaped to her small head, and a new jersey dress showing off the slender lines of her figure.

Sheila smiled back brightly at her daughter, and then turned as James came in. 'James, darling, do tell me all about Cyndy Burnett,' she begged, sitting down in the armchair by the fire. 'Is she really as lovely as she is on stage? She looked so sweet in that musical you took me to see. And what's her flat like? I'm dying to hear all about it.'

Rosalind and James smiled at each other. They were always careful not to talk too much about their clients, but it was surprising how much information you could keep back, while appearing to be forthcoming. The colour of a pair of curtains didn't seem to be too confidential, and Sheila would be happy enough knowing about that, while any more private knowledge could be retained. Both were aware of being in a privileged position with regard to their clients and would never have dreamed of gossiping about them.

The rest of the evening passed pleasantly enough. Sheila served a delicious *bouillabaisse*, followed by apple tart, and they returned to the fireside to drink their coffee.

Encouraged by their interest, she told them

all the local news and it was not until later that she returned to the subject of their careers. 'I've been telling our newest arrival all about you,' she said, passing a dish of mints. 'Remember I told you that Stret Barn had been sold? Rather an attractive man—single, apparently, though nobody knows much about him yet. I met him at a cocktail party recently and he told me he intends to completely restore it and live there. A nice little job for someone there.'

'That's if he intends to call in professionals,' James said, stretching his long legs to the fire. 'Some people like to do it themselves. No consideration for starving interior decorators, but there you are. It's a free country.'

'Does he intend to do it himself?' Rosalind asked. She was feeling sleepy after the long day at work, the stressful drive through the fog and the meal. Sitting in front of the fire with James on a big, comfortable sofa, she felt more interested in falling asleep than in discussing the furnishings of the barn that stood on the edge of the village.

Sheila sipped her coffee. 'I'm not sure. I asked him, and mentioned you as I said, but he just smiled and said he hadn't decided on anything yet. Rather an enigmatic character, I thought.' She sounded faintly aggrieved. 'Anyway, you'll meet him, I've asked a few people in for drinks tomorrow evening. Mostly people you know, but there'll be Troy—that's his name, Troy Ballard, unusual isn't it?—oh yes, and another newcomer to the village.' She held out her hand for their cups and busied herself pouring more coffee. 'Rather a nice man, actually—a retired brigadier. Brigadier Maynard. He's bought Highmeadow—that rather nice Georgian house on the Stow road.'

'Highmeadow? And doesn't he want it completely refurbished?' James asked quizzically, and Sheila shook her head at him.

'Don't be naughty, James. Though I agree that would be a real plum. But Highmeadow's always been kept beautifully—the old couple who lived there treated it like a precious jewel. I don't think it needs a thing doing to it.'

Rosalind put up her hand to stifle a yawn. 'Don't pour me any more coffee, Mother. I think I'll go to bed. I can hardly keep my eyes open and I want to be fresh in the morning for all the things you've planned.'

Things I could well do without, she thought as she went up to the bedroom under the eaves. Why couldn't her mother just let them have a restful weekend, doing absolutely nothing for once? But no, she always had to organise everything. A morning's shopping here, coffee there, lunch somewhere else, tea with friends, drinks in the evening ... 'And that's just Saturday,' she told James when he joined her in the big bed. 'I haven't dared ask about Sunday.'

He laughed. 'Perhaps you could develop a

headache. Stay in bed, enjoy a bit of cossetting. Sheila would be delighted to look after you.'

'Don't tempt me.' She snuggled against him. 'Anyway, it wouldn't work—Mother's always known when I'm lying. And if she did believe me, you know what it would be like: first of all she wouldn't want me going back to London in the evening and then she'd be ringing every day to see how I was. It wouldn't be worth it. I'll have a headache next weekend instead.'

James slipped his arms around her and drew her close. 'Don't do that,' he murmured, his lips almost touching hers. 'You know how I worry about your headaches.'

'Oh, you!' she retorted, though her heart was already beginning to race. 'All you worry about is...' But his lips were teasing hers and she couldn't finish. She felt his hands straying over her body, one on her breast, the other stroking very gently down her spine so that she gasped and moved against him.

'Yes?' he whispered, flicking his tongue gently across her mouth. 'What is it I worry about? Tell me.'

'James ... oh, James...' He was close against her now, his arm tightening around her so that she could feel the long, warm length of him. Her own arms were winding around his neck, her mouth returning his kiss, her lips and tongue tangling with his as they lay clasped together. And there was now nothing she wanted to say to him. All their communication, all their love was being expressed through the medium of touch, of closeness, of tender passion. Neither needed words of any kind.

Three years married, she thought as she returned James's loving, and it gets better all the time. We'll never lose this, never. Whatever happens, we shall always love each other this way.

The last shred of unhappiness over their quarrel faded away. How could it ever have marred what they had? How could she let it happen again?

Safe in her husband's arms, Rosalind determined that nothing would ever be allowed to come between them.

*   *   *

'... and this is Brigadier Maynard. Richard, this is my daughter, Rosalind Camarthey.' There was a slight flush on her mother's cheeks, Rosalind noticed as she was introduced to the tall, upright man with iron-grey hair and bright blue eyes who could have been nothing other than a soldier. A small moustache bristled on his upper lip and he looked as if he had been polished. But his manner was pleasant enough and his handshake firm.

'Glad to meet you, Mrs Camarthey. Hear you're an interior decorator. Work in London,

don't you?'

'Yes, that's right, for Lords & Ladies—you might have heard of them.' His blank expression told her that he hadn't, but she decided he wasn't the sort of man who would have heard of any interior decorating firm. 'And please call me Rosalind. If you're a friend of my mother's—'

'Well, I hope I can call myself that.' The grey moustache bristled. 'Only known her for a few weeks, you understand, but we seemed to hit it off right from the start.' He cleared his throat. 'Fine woman. Very much a lady.'

'Yes,' Rosalind murmured, rather at a loss as to how she should respond to this. There was a short silence. She cast around for a new topic of conversation and was just about to ask how long he had been retired from the Army when she saw, over his shoulder, the door open and another man walk in.

His eyes met hers instantly—almost, she thought, as if he had been looking for her, and the words died on Rosalind's lips.

Brigadier Maynard turned to see what she was looking at. 'Ah, this is someone else you haven't met!' he exclaimed. 'Let me introduce you—Ballard, this is Mrs Mitchell's daughter, Rosalind Camarthey. Mrs Cam—er, Rosalind—this is another new neighbour, Troy Ballard. Bought that old barn on the edge of the village, the one that used to belong to—'

'Yes, I know it.' Rosalind held out her hand,

30

moving almost as if she were an automaton, and felt Troy Ballard take it in his. His clasp was warm and strong and when he released her she drew back thankfully. 'My mother told me you intend to restore it.'

'That's right.' Troy Ballard's voice was deep. His eyes held hers, a bright grey, almost silver. He was tall—as tall as James—with hair the colour of ripe corn under a hot summer sun. He was impossibly handsome and Rosalind felt an instant and instinctive distrust of him. 'And you're the lady who's going to help me choose wallpaper,' he went on, his eyes alive with amusement. 'Isn't that right, Brigadier?'

The old soldier coughed. 'Wouldn't know about that. Understand she's very talented—very much in demand. Works in London, y'know.'

'Well, I know where London is,' Troy said with a smile. 'And I'm willing to join the queue. You'll have to give me your card, Rosalind.'

Rosalind glanced wildly around. Where was James? Didn't he know she needed him? 'I think my husband's more likely to be the one you need,' she stammered. 'He deals more with out of town assignments. I tend to concentrate on properties in Town.'

'Oh, that's a pity.' Troy helped himself to a drink from a nearby table. 'I'd have enjoyed discussing my plans with you. Still, there it is, you can't win 'em all.' He smiled, showing perfect teeth. 'Perhaps if I asked for you

31

specially? No? Oh well, no doubt you'll be coming down to visit your mother from time to time. We're bound to meet again. Now, if you'll excuse me, there's someone over there I must talk to.'

He gave them both another smile and drifted away, moving easily about the room as if he were perfectly at home and exchanging a few words with everyone he passed along the way.

The person he had to talk to, Rosalind noticed, was a girl she had been at school with. Samantha Curtis. Very glamorous. They'd never been real friends but Sheila invariably asked her to any party she gave when Rosalind was home. She was looking more exotic than ever tonight and greeted Troy Ballard with a possessive smile, linking her arm in his at once.

Rosalind turned back to the Brigadier and began to ask him about his travels.

* * *

'Thank goodness that's over,' Rosalind said, settling herself in the passenger seat as James swung the car out on to the main road. 'I thought the weekend would never end.'

'Oh, it wasn't so bad.' James pulled out to overtake a slow van. 'Went rather well, I thought. Not a blow exchanged; not even a heated argument. You both behaved admirably.'

'Honestly, James! You make it sound as if

Mother and I are always at each other's throats. We're not at all. You know we think the world of each other. She just—well—'

'Drives you mad?' he suggested helpfully.

'I was going to say *irritates* me, at times. That's all it is. And only when she starts to treat me like a little girl. But I suppose most mothers are like that with their children. They never quite accept the fact that their baby's grown up.'

'I wouldn't know,' James said thoughtfully, 'only having one mother myself.'

'Well, your mother's different, I know that. And there being so many of you must make a difference.'

'Not that many,' he protested. 'She wasn't the old woman who lived in a shoe, you know. She can count all of us on the fingers of one hand.' He thought for a moment, then added, 'Just.'

'Well, five is a big family—especially when you compare it with one. And she's always had your father around, too. Mother's only ever had me.'

'Yes,' he said gently, taking his hand from the wheel to lay it over hers. 'And I think we ought to remember that a little more. It's almost impossible to imagine what it must be like to lose your husband the day before your baby is born. It must have had a terrible effect, one she's never really got over.'

Rosalind was silent. She had often thought

of her father when she was a child, trying to picture him, imagining what it would have been like if he had been alive to play with her, to teach her to ride a bike, to take her swimming. Somehow, she had never wondered how it had been for her mother, left alone to bring up a baby, left without a husband to share the problems, the worries, the joys.

The loving.

That had been something that Rosalind, as a child, had never been aware of. And since she'd grown up she'd been too busy to give it much thought at all. She'd been accustomed to the situation, and assumed that her mother was too. After all, there must have been chances for her to marry again if she'd wanted to. She was attractive enough, she had friends, an active social life. If she hadn't, it must surely have been because she just wasn't interested.

But had she missed it? The kind of closeness that Rosalind shared with James—the passion, the tenderness, the sharing? Had it left a void in her life?

Rosalind turned away from her uncomfortable thoughts. 'What did you think of the Brigadier?' she asked James quickly, and caught his grin.

'Oh, marvellous. I couldn't take my eyes off him. If ever I saw anyone who couldn't be anything other than what he is, that man's the Brigadier. And definitely interested in your mother. Wedding bells there, I shouldn't

34

wonder.'

'Wedding bells?' Rosalind turned her head to stare at him. 'James, don't be ridiculous!'

'Ridiculous? What's ridiculous about that?'

'Well...' She struggled for words. 'It just *is*, that's all. I mean—Mother and the Brigadier! Surely you can see that.'

'No,' James said after a moment, 'I can't, I'm afraid. It seems quite suitable to me. And certainly possible.'

'*Suitable?* But he's years older than Mother.'

'Ten, perhaps. That's nothing. I'm eight years older than you.'

'And she's been on her own for twenty-six years. If she'd been going to marry again she'd have done it long ago. I mean, thinking about it now, after all these years—it's just silly.'

'Silly? Why?' There was an odd note in James's voice. They were on a straight road now, without much traffic, and he was free to talk easily. 'Ros, your mother's a relatively young woman, still. Why shouldn't she have a little happiness?'

'But she does have happiness! She's got her shop, her cottage, her friends—what more does she need?' She caught James's raised eyebrows and felt her face flush. 'James, don't! It's my mother you're talking about.'

'Who presumably doesn't have the needs and desires the rest of us do,' he said. 'Grow up, Rosalind.'

Rosalind gasped. How dared he speak to her

like that? She said, coldly, 'I'm well aware of the facts of life, thank you, James. I'm not so immature as to imagine that they don't apply to my own mother. But she's managed quite happily all these years without a man. I don't see why she has to throw up everything she has at this stage, for a man like the Brigadier—'

'And you know, of course, just what kind of man he is. You've talked to him for—oh, all of ten minutes. And with your famous ability to judge a person on the strength of ten minutes' conversation, you know all about him. His likes and dislikes, his temperament, his romantic past, his—'

'*James!* Stop it!' To her fury, she felt the tears come to her eyes, heard them in her voice. 'It's my mother you're talking about,' she repeated angrily. '*My mother*. Don't you understand what that means? Don't you have any idea—'

'Yes, I think I do.' To her astonishment, she realised that he was as angry as she. He swung the car suddenly into a layby at the side of the road, braked and then turned to face her. 'Listen to me, Rosalind. You talk very glibly about *your mother*, as if she's some kind or rare, endangered species. She's a woman, Rosalind, a woman just like you. More like you, I think, than you realise. She has the same needs, the same feelings, the same desires. How dare you say that she's managed "quite happily" all these years without a man? How

36

do *you* know she's been happy? And now that there does seem to be a chance of her finding someone she can care for, you react as though someone's suggested something disgusting. You know what I think? I think you're jealous.'

'*Jealous*?' Rosalind gasped, and he nodded.

'Yes, jealous. Jealous because you want her all to yourself. You want her there whenever you need her, whenever you deign to pay a visit. You don't want anyone else in her life, competing with you for her attention. You're jealous and possessive, Ros, and it's time you grew out of it.'

For a few moments, Rosalind found herself unable to speak. She stared at her husband in the dimness of the car. She could see his face, taut with anger, and she shook her head unbelievingly. How could he say these things to her? How could he even think them? Surely he knew her better than that? Or was he, too, a stranger?

'You're talking nonsense,' she whispered at last. 'You know none of that's true. *Me*, possessive? It's Mother who's possessive. She's the one who wants me to come and visit, who complains if I don't ring her at least once a week. She's the one who won't let me alone, who treats me like a baby, her little girl—'

'And you,' James said quietly, 'are the one who revels in that treatment. Yes, you do, Ros—you aid and abet her, all along the way.

Oh, you might pretend you resent it, you might grumble about having to visit, you might be reluctant to ring, but you do it just the same. You like the feeling that you're the most important person in her life—just as you like to feel that you're the most important person in mine.'

'But I am,' she whispered, and then, shaken by sudden doubt, 'aren't I?'

James's face softened. He put up his hand and stroked her cheek with gentle fingers. 'Of course you are, Ros. But until you get rid of this—this attachment to your mother, you'll never be properly yourself. You'll both be tied together, each one unable to move without the other, and it's not healthy. You've got to get over it, Ros. For her sake. For your own sake. And for the sake of our marriage.'

He turned away and started the car again. They drove into the night, away from the countryside where Rosalind had grown up, back to the lights of London. And Rosalind sat silent all the way, trying to come to terms with James's words and fighting them, pushing them away, refusing to believe that there could be any truth in them.

Jealous? Possessive? Tied to her mother? It wasn't true. None of it was true. It was just too ridiculous even to contemplate. James had got it all wrong. And that hurt more than anything he had said, because for all this time she had imagined he understood her. And she saw now that he did not understand the first thing about her.

* * *

Rosalind had still not spoken when they came into the flat together. She waited for James to unlock the door, walked past him and crossed to the window. She stared out at the lights for a few moments, then drew the curtains. She was aware of James crossing the room behind her, standing at her shoulder, but she stubbornly refused to turn her head.

'Ros,' he said quietly in her ear. 'Ros, look at me.' He waited a moment. 'Well, then listen to me. Please.'

'I can hardly do anything else,' she said coldly, 'but I can't imagine what else you can have to say.'

She heard him sigh, then felt his hand on her shoulder. 'Ros, please. Don't let's quarrel over this. I know you didn't like what I said about you and your mother, but they're things I've been thinking for a long time. Things I believe needed to be said. But I would never have said them, any of them, if I didn't love you. Can't you understand that? Can't you believe it?'

She whipped round, facing him with eyes that burned blue, like coals on a frosty night. 'Believe it? Understand it? James, I don't know what you're talking about. You say all those cruel, horrible things and you ask me to believe that you say them because you love me? How can I believe that? It's crazy—it's grotesque!' To her fury, she felt the tears coming. She tried to hold them back, then covered her face with her hands, turning away from him so that he would not see. But James caught her shoulders and turned her back, making her face him.

'Ros, *listen* to me. What horrible things have I said? Only that you're too attached to your mother, that's all. It's not a crime. Yes, you're jealous and possessive, both of you, but it's natural enough in the circumstances and you can overcome it. And I want you to, because I love you—because I care about you both, but most of all because I love *you*, Ros. I want you to be the full, whole person you are deep inside, the person you can be once you shake off your childhood and become the real Ros. I'm not asking you to do anything unkind or unnatural. It will be good for both of you. You both need to be free of each other, to live your own lives.'

Rosalind lowered her hands and stared at him. 'Free?' she said, her voice shaking. 'Live our own lives? But we do already. We *are* free. Do you know what I think, James, in this childish, jealous, possessive brain of mine? I think it's *you* who have never grown up. It's *you* who are jealous and possessive. Not me at all. *You!*' She paused, trembling, then continued in a voice that grew dull and quiet as she spoke, as she heard herself uttering words she had never dreamed would be spoken

40

between them. 'I don't believe you love me at all,' she whispered. 'I don't believe you ever did. Not really.' And now the tears came in earnest and she turned away from him, shaken by a storm of sobbing that tore her from head to foot.

James touched her once, but she wrenched herself away from him. She heard him move away, heard the soft sigh of the cushions as he threw himself on to the sofa. Then the room was silent except for the sound of her own weeping.

At last, however, the storm began to abate. The tears began to dry, the painful sobs ceased to rip from her breast. She lifted her face from her hands and found James once more at her side. And now she allowed him to take her in his arms.

'There,' he murmured, as if he were soothing an unhappy child. 'It's all right, Ros, darling. It's all right. Don't cry any more. Please don't cry any more. It's all all right.'

She looked at him. Her eyes felt swollen and heavy, and she knew they must be red and ugly in a face that was blotched with weeping. She shook her head, exhausted and bewildered. For a few minutes, she couldn't even remember what they had quarrelled about. 'I'm not jealous and possessive,' she whispered at last. 'I'm not childish, James—I'm not.'

'It's all right,' he soothed her. 'Don't think about it any more now. Let me make you a cup

41

of tea and then you can go to bed. You're worn out.'

'I'm not,' she repeated as he led her to the bedroom and tenderly helped her to undress. 'I'm not ... I'm not...'

'Look,' James said, 'here's your favourite nightie, the one with the blue ribbons. Let's get it on you and then I'll go and fetch that tea. That's it—into bed now.' He covered her with the duvet and looked down at her. 'Oh darling, I hate to see you so upset. I really do. I love you so much.'

Rosalind looked up at him. There was something familiar in the scene, as if she had taken part in it before, although not with James. Someone else had once stood beside her like this, had said words that sounded very similar. She tried to remember, failed, and turned her head on the pillow. She felt suddenly very, very tired.

James left the room and Rosalind heard the sound of the kettle being filled in the small, white kitchen. She lay very quiet, looking up at the ceiling. And then it came back to her.

A memory from twenty years ago. Herself, coming in crying because of some squabble with her best friend. Her mother soothing her, comforting her, putting her to bed. Across the years, Rosalind heard the echo of her voice.

'*Look. Here's your favourite nightie—the one with the blue ribbons. Let's get it on you and then I'll bring you some hot milk.*'

The tears began again. And when James came back with the tray of tea, Rosalind was lying face down on her pillow, shaking with sobs and repeating over and over again: 'I'm not ... I'm not ... I'm not ...'

CHAPTER THREE

Christmas was drawing near. The trees in Oxford Street twinkled with lights and the new display had been switched on in Regent Street. The pavements were crowded with people— some racing along as if their lives depended on reaching their destination on time, some dawdling past the big shop windows, admiring the tableaux of Father Christmas, Snow White and other seasonal characters. Christmas was the word on everyone's lips—Happy Christmas! Have you done all your Christmas shopping yet? Are you ready for Christmas? As if it were some once-in-a-lifetime event, Rosalind thought, rather than something which happened every year.

She and James were going to his family after all. Sheila had been surprisingly acquiescent when Ros had broached the subject, saying only in a martyred tone that she supposed there would be a big gathering at the Camartheys', and it would be a shame to miss it. 'Not needing to mention that she'll be all alone,'

Rosalind said to James as she put down the phone. 'Oh dear ... I wish now I'd said we'd go to her ...'

'Which is exactly what she wants you to wish.' James came over and laid his hands on her shoulders. 'Ros, you know she'll be perfectly happy. She's got plenty of friends, she'll be invited to every meal possible for the whole week and have a whale of a time. She knows it and you know it. In fact, if you *had* said we'd go, she would probably have been quite put out. She's just going through the motions.'

'D'you really think so?' Rosalind asked doubtfully, and he laughed and hugged her.

'I'm sure so. Now, let's dress the tree.' He moved away and began to unpack the gold and silver artificial tree Rosalind had brought home. 'Shame we can't have a real one, but I see your point—they're not really very convenient.'

'Oh, they're not nearly so good.' The tree had come supplied with all its own baubles and decorations. 'Dropping needles everywhere, you're sweeping them up for months afterwards. And it's so difficult to get one with a good shape.' She admired the symmetrical lines of the glittering tree. 'This looks lovely.'

'It certainly goes well with the room,' James agreed. 'I'd recommend it to any client. Well, any client who has a white and gold room like ours, of course.' He hesitated for a moment.

44

'Ros...'

'Mmm? Oh, hold this crystal chain for me, will you?' Rosalind wound the delicate, glittering chain of beads around the branches. 'There. What were you going to say?'

'Oh ... nothing.' He frowned a little, then said, 'Next year, perhaps we'll stay at home for Christmas.'

'Stay at home? Here?' Rosalind looked round the room with the tasteful, discreet decorations they had chosen. 'But you love going to your family for Christmas. And you like going to Mother's too ... don't you? The carols and parties and everything?'

'Oh yes, I enjoy them both. I like all the traditions, you know that. I just think—well, maybe it's time to start a few traditions of our own.'

'Well, yes, it would be nice to do that,' Rosalind said a little doubtfully. 'Though I don't know quite what traditions we could start. I can't quite imagine us here for Christmas, James, with everyone else away. Nobody we know stays in London, they all go away.'

'I know. That's—' He stopped and grinned at her. 'Well, never mind, we haven't had this Christmas yet, let alone started to think about the next. Who knows what will have happened by then? Our lives might be completely different.'

Rosalind looked at him and then came to

stand close. Almost tentatively, she reached out to touch his face. 'You're not thinking about a family, are you, James? You know we agreed to wait five years.'

He looked down at her and his hand came up to cover hers. 'I know. And it wasn't what I was thinking of. But there's something we ought to discuss, Ros—something else.'

'Something important?' she asked, and he nodded.

'I think so, yes.'

Rosalind looked at him. His face was serious and she felt a sudden tremor. Whatever it was, she didn't want to know about it. It was Christmas—a time for enjoyment, for laughter and fun and happiness. Not a time for serious discussion. 'Does it have to be now?' she asked in a small voice.

'It doesn't have to be, no. It can wait till after Christmas.'

'Then let's leave it till then.' She tossed back her hair, laughing at him. Dear James! He took life so seriously at times. And this couldn't possibly be so very important, if it could wait until after Christmas. Why, by then it might be quite forgotten.

She spun away from him and stopped again by the tree, drinking in its glittering beauty. 'Tell me after Christmas,' she said over her shoulder. 'I can't think about anything else till then. There's so much to be done still—all the wrapping and the cards, and I still haven't got

Cyndy Burnett to finalise on the bathroom. Do you know, she actually wants gold taps! I've tried to tell her, *nobody* has gold taps any more but she won't listen. Honestly, if her public could see what she's really like! That sweet image definitely turns sour when it comes to dealing with the serfs—and that's how she sees us, you know. I'll be thankful when this job's over.'

'Never mind, it's a good job and when Cyndy's flat is featured in one of the glossy monthlies, Lords & Ladies will get a nice plug.' James fitted the gossamer-clad porcelain fairy to the top of the tree. 'There. Now all we need is a few beautifully-wrapped parcels underneath and the illusion is complete.'

There was an odd note in his voice as he said the last words, and Rosalind turned to look at him. But James was looking soberly at the tree and his face gave nothing away. After a moment, he turned back to her and she saw with relief that he was smiling again. 'That's it! Now let's have a drink to celebrate the beginning of Christmas.'

'The beginning of Christmas,' Rosalind said, holding up the glass he gave her, and they wound their free arms around each other's waists and drank together.

All the same, she couldn't help wondering just what was in his mind—what it was he wanted to discuss with her. But again, she pushed the thoughts away. Wait until after

47

Christmas, she told herself. Don't think about anything else.

Don't let anything spoil this.

*   *   *

They went down to James's home in north Hampshire on Christmas Eve. It was cold, with a hint of snow blowing in the air, and the villages they drove through were bright with Christmas trees on greens and in front windows. Tiny shops were strung with coloured lights, their windows crammed with huge boxes of chocolates which were being removed for last-minute buyers even as Rosalind and James passed, and children wrapped in anoraks and scarves ran and skipped along the streets, their bodies taut with excitement.

'It's like a Christmas card everywhere,' Rosalind observed as they came at last to the village where James's father practised as doctor. She looked up at the big, plain-fronted house with its Christmas wreath on the door and the welcome shining from its windows. 'It's so different from London. I wouldn't be surprised to hear real carol singers.'

'Oh, they'll have been round all the week.' James leaned into the car and emerged with an armful of parcels. 'They'll be saving their voices now for the midnight service and tomorrow morning. I'm always surprised they can sing at all by Christmas Day. Take this stuff, will you, Ros? It's too cold to keep making trips out to collect things.'

Laden with luggage and parcels, they staggered to the front door and were relieved to see it fly open just before they reached it. A tumble of children erupted over the threshold, and behind them Rosalind saw the smiling faces of James's parents, with his brothers and sisters in the background. A warm smell of punch and mince pies drifted out, and then they were engulfed in welcoming arms and drawn into the warmth.

And warmth, Rosalind later decided, was the keynote of Christmas with the Camartheys. It was there from the very beginning—in the glow that streamed from that open front door; in the faces that beamed on her and James as they were almost manhandled into the hall, relieved of their burdens and soundly hugged and kissed; in the log fires that blazed in every possible fireplace; in the huge Christmas tree that glittered with colourful decorations in the corner; and in the supper that was served round a big kitchen table to a family that never stopped talking or laughing.

And in Christmas Day itself, with the excitement of present-giving, the turkey dinner, the walk in the afternoon across frosty fields (the snow having failed to fall) and the return to tea and Christmas cake by the fire, games with the children and, much later, a

49

buffet supper that was demolished surprisingly quickly considering that everyone had declared themselves only a few hours earlier as being too full to need food for at least another three days.

'You're just a lot of gluttons,' James's mother declared as she watched them bearing away laden plates. 'Still, at least it means I haven't wasted my time in preparing it all. Not that I did prepare it all,' she added to Rosalind. 'The girls all contributed something and that enormous ham you brought will feed even this horde for several meals. Now, bring your plate and come and sit in my corner with me, and we'll talk. I've hardly had a moment to exchange a word with you all Christmas.'

Rosalind laughed. 'How you can say that, when we've never stopped talking!' But she gathered up her plate of cold meat and salad and followed Anna Camarthey to her 'corner'—a cosy cluster of armchairs and stools in what had once been a big cupboard, opened up to form an alcove off the living room. This was Anna's own little domain, where she sat when she wanted to be quiet or to talk with just one or two of her family. Not only was it respected as such, but it was considered by her children and grandchildren to be something of an honour to be invited into it.

'Now, tell me all about life in London. Are you still happy there?' Anna had never believed in beating about the bush, but her questions were always kind and never intrusive.

Rosalind smiled at her and nodded. 'Yes, very happy.' She hesitated, remembering the quarrels she and James had had lately, then nodded again more positively. 'Very happy indeed. It's all perfect.'

'That's good.' But Anna's gaze was speculative. 'I was never sure if James would settle in London. But with the right person, I think one settles anywhere, don't you? And I've never had any doubt but that you're the right person for James.'

Rosalind looked down at her plate, feeling a sudden mist of tears. *Was* she the right person for James? She'd never doubted that he was right for her—but she never lost the faint, niggling fear that he might have found someone better, that she didn't quite satisfy him...

'Of course,' Anna said absently, as if talking to herself, 'nobody finds marriage perfect all the time. It really is fraught with problems, and it doesn't get any easier as time goes on either. There are still times when I could cheerfully wrap Robert's stethoscope round his neck and strangle him with it. And then I think—why should I spend the rest of my life in a prison cell, when with a little patience I can have all this!' And she looked around the comfortable room, the happy faces, and made a comical face at Rosalind.

51

Rosalind laughed, and found James at her elbow, his own plate almost overflowing.

'Is this a private party, or can anyone join in?'

'Not anyone, no,' his mother returned, 'but I daresay we'll make an exception in your case, shall we, Ros?'

'Oh, I think so.' She felt her husband's presence like an added warmth beside her and added impulsively, 'You know, this is what Christmas is all about. Families being together. And this is such a lovely house to have it in, too. It has such a warm atmosphere.'

'In spite of the decor?' Anna murmured wickedly, and Rosalind laughed again.

'Well, it isn't what James or I would design for a client,' she admitted. 'We would never even think of putting all the things together that you have. It's such a mixture. But it all works. It comes together, somehow, as if it were meant.'

'That's because everything has its own meaning; its own associations,' Anna told her. 'None of it has been added because it matches the rest—everything in this room has been collected haphazardly on our journey through life, but it all meant something to us when we acquired it, and it still has that meaning. It's a part of ourselves—our personalities. Mine, Robert's and each of the children—we all brought something to this house that made it a home, and so it can't help but blend together.'

'Yes, I see that,' Rosalind said slowly. 'And that's something James and I can never do for our clients—make them a home. That's something they have to do for themselves.' She stared pensively into the fire, then added only half-jokingly, 'I think I'll give up interior decorating and go in for—oh, running a souvenir shop instead!'

James and Anna laughed, but Anna seemed to catch the slightly despondent note in Rosalind's voice and leaned forward to touch her knee.

'Don't be disheartened, my dear. Your clients know just what they want when they come to you and you give it to them. You're giving them a setting—something to start from. What they do with it after that is up to them. Their touches will make it a home—but they can't do it without you. And if they don't want to turn your setting into their home— well, isn't that up to them?'

'Of course it is,' James declared before Rosalind could answer. 'We're providing a service, that's all, not running a counselling bureau. Now—do you want any more salad, Ros, or shall I bring you both some of Juliet's sumptuous hazelnut meringue? She brings it every Christmas and stands over us with an axe if we don't eat it all up.'

'Precious little chance there is of that,' Rosalind observed. 'I've tasted Juliet's hazelnut meringue before. Yes, please, but not too much or I won't be able to get into that new dress for the party tomorrow night.' She watched James depart towards the kitchen and smiled at her mother-in-law.

'It's quite obvious that you and James are very happy,' Anna said. 'And how do you feel about this new job he's been offered?'

Rosalind's smile froze on her lips. 'New ... job? I don't—'

'Oh, my dear!' Anna looked appalled. 'Don't say he hasn't told you! Oh, I *am* sorry—I should never have mentioned it if I'd realised. I thought he'd been sure to have—he did say it was only an idea, maybe he decided against it, but all the same—Rosalind, don't look like that. I'm sure he intended to discuss it with you—'

It was the first time Rosalind had ever seen her mother-in-law flustered. They gazed at each other, unable to say any more, until James returned with the plates of meringue. Rosalind took hers mechanically and stared at it. Meringue? New job? Christmas? Suddenly everything had lost its savour.

But there was no chance then to ask James what it was all about. It was Christmas, and the children were clamouring for charades. And within a few minutes, they were dragged out of Anna's corner and made to arrange their chairs with the others in front of a makeshift stage, made to act out words and guess the titles of films and plays and books, made to laugh and

54

sing and be merry until the grandfather clock in the corner had long since struck midnight. Made to smile at each other, to kiss under the mistletoe and finally to put the guard in front of the smouldering fire and go upstairs to bed, too tired to do more than wish each other a last good-night before falling asleep in the big double bed in the room that had once been a nursery.

But although she fell asleep quickly, Rosalind did not sleep for long. After two or three hours, she was awake, staring into the darkness, wondering why the window was in the wrong place. And remembering what Anna had said to her, downstairs in her corner. *How do you feel about the new job James has been offered? How do you feel about the new job ... the new job ... the new job ...?*

How could he not have discussed it with her? After all he had said when she had turned down Brent Woodford's offer—how could he not have told her?

What new job was it anyway? Did he intend to accept it? And if he did—what effect would it have on them? On their relationship?

On the marriage that Anna thought was so happy?

*   *   *

The drive home was silent, the atmosphere tense. Rosalind sat in the passenger seat, staring into the fog that surrounded them like a cocoon of dirty cotton wool. It was impossible to talk to James in these conditions—he needed all his concentration to get them home safely. But she knew she could not keep silent for much longer.

She had said nothing yet about Anna's revelation, but it had scarcely left her mind during the seemingly endless Boxing Day, with its yawning late start, the clearing up of wrapping paper and nutshells, the brisk walk across the fields and the late lunch of turkey soup, baked potatoes and cold meats and cheeses.

Always, there had been people around them—James's brothers and sisters with their wives and husbands, the children who cavorted and tumbled about like so many puppies, and Robert and Anna themselves who had worked so hard to make this a really happy family Christmas, and must not be hurt by unseasonal quarrels.

It had been impossible to talk quietly with James. She had not even been able to hint at what was troubling her. All the same, her knowledge had caused a rift between them. Try as she might to be cheerful, to appear happy and carefree, she had been unable to stop the thoughts circling in her brain, and she knew James was aware of something wrong.

At last they were home. They parked the car and went up to their flat, laden now with the presents they had been given. They took everything into the bedroom and piled it in a corner, and then went back to the living room for a drink. Rosalind sank down in a corner of the sofa and rested her head on one hand.

'Right,' James said, setting a glass on the small table beside her, 'now you can tell me what's the matter.'

It was what she'd been wanting to do for the past forty-eight hours. Yet now, unreasonably, she felt angry that he had to ask. Perhaps it was the pent-up anger of the past two days that had to be released. She turned to him and her voice was scathing. 'Matter? Whatever makes you think something's the matter?'

James stared at her, his eyes narrowed. 'Come on, Ros. You know perfectly well you've been like a bear with a sore head ever since Christmas night—'

'I have *not!*'

'—and you've been just longing to get me on my own so that you can let rip. So—'

'Get you on your own!' she interrupted with a bitter laugh. 'That's a joke! It's impossible to get anyone on their own in that house—there are people everywhere, and most of them children. In corners, in the middle of the floor, using the table, racing up and down the stairs—'

'Is that what it is?' he asked. 'Do the children get on your nerves? Does my whole family get on your nerves? I thought you liked them, Ros.

I thought you were going to enjoy Christmas with them. In fact, until late on Christmas night I believed you *were* enjoying it.'

'Yes, I was,' she admitted after a moment. 'And it's not your family. It's not the children—they're dears, all of them, even when they get over-excited. It's nothing to do with Christmas.'

'Then why? What is it? Because I know something's wrong, Ros, and we have to sort it out. You have to let me help.'

Her anger welled up again. 'Let you help? James, don't you realise, you *caused* it! It's all because of you.' To her fury, she realised she was going to start crying. 'Oh, why did you do it?' she wept. 'Why did you take another job without even consulting me—*and then tell your mother about it first*? Why?'

James stared at her. She looked back at him, challenging him to deny it. He ran his hand through his hair, opened his mouth to speak, closed it again. 'Oh, lor',' he said at last, and picked up his glass.

'Well, is that all you can say?' Rosalind demanded. 'Don't you think I'm entitled to some sort of explanation?'

'Yes,' he said, 'of course you are. Ros, I'm sorry. I never meant you to find out like that. I was going to talk to you—tell you all about it—but there was never time—'

'Never time? You found time to tell your mother.'

'Yes, I know, but that wasn't meant to happen either. It was when I was helping her get the turkey out of the oven—you know what a size it was, she couldn't manage it on her own and she won't have people in the kitchen when she's doing that, says it's dangerous—'

'Well, it is,' Rosalind admitted. 'All that hot fat and everything. But why tell her about a new job just then? I'd have thought you were too busy with what you were doing.'

'Yes, we were, in a way. It just—came up.' He gazed at her. 'Don't look like that, Ros. It just happens that Mum knows the man who offered me the job. He's a neighbour of theirs. And she knows what business he's in, of course, and just mentioned his name—asked me if I ever ran across him. And I said yes, I'd seen him only last week and he'd ... offered me a job.'

There was a short silence.

'I see,' Rosalind said at last. 'So you and your mother had a nice, cosy chat about it out there in the kitchen. And it all came up by accident. Are you sure there wasn't more to it than that, James?'

'How do you mean, more to it? What more could there be?'

'Well, it seems a strange coincidence that Anna just happens to know this man and just happened to mention him to you, and you'd just happened to have met him and been offered a job by him. I just wondered if there

59

wasn't a bit more to it. Like, she mentioned you to him, for example.'

'Oh, don't be ridiculous! Of course there was nothing like that. I don't need my mother to find jobs for me. It was just that, Ros—a coincidence. And I'm sorry I didn't mention it to you first but I wanted to sort my own thoughts out—'

'*Mention* it?' she broke in. 'I'd have thought you'd do more than *mention* it. What happened to "discussion"? Wasn't that what you wanted when I was offered a job a few weeks ago? Didn't it ever occur to you that I was entitled to discussion, to consultation, as well? Or doesn't that sort of thing work both ways? I thought we had a partnership, James, but maybe I was wrong. Maybe you just want to be in charge and make all the decisions, about my work and yours, like some Victorian patriarch.'

'It's not like that at all—' James began, but Rosalind interrupted again.

She was trembling with anger now, aware that her voice was growing shriller but unable to stop it. The angry thoughts that had circled in her head for the past two days were fighting each other to come to the surface, and it was almost impossible to know which ones to voice first.

'Not like that? Well, tell me what it is like then. I'd be really interested to know what it's like when a man gets an offer of a job and doesn't get around to mentioning it to his wife

60

before he discusses it with his mother—'

'We didn't discuss it! Ros, you're blowing this up out of all proportion.'

'Am I? Am I? Well, tell me what proportion it ought to be in, then. Just tell me about it, James.'

'I will, if you'll just stop shouting for a few minutes and give me a chance.' He was as angry as she now, and they glared at each other for a moment, both breathing heavily, their fists clenched. Then James made a visible effort to relax.

He turned away, picked up his drink again and sipped. He looked at Rosalind's glass. 'A top-up?'

'Yes, please,' she muttered and he picked up the bottle and refilled their glasses. Then he sipped again before setting his drink carefully back on the little table.

'Right. Now if you'll just let me tell you quietly. I was approached last week by a head-hunter—you know what a head-hunter is, don't you?'

'Someone who tries to entice people away from their jobs with the offer of a better one,' she said impatiently. 'Of *course* I know what a head-hunter is. I don't spend all my time in a hole in the ground, James.'

'All right, all right. Anyway, this guy asked me out for lunch—it was the day you were with Cyndy Burnett—and he told me that IntInt were looking for someone to head a new design team. He said they wanted to consider me. And I—'

'*IntInt*?' Rosalind exclaimed. 'Interiors International? But—they're one of the biggest firms of designers in Europe—'

'I know.'

She caught the note in his voice and gave him a sharp glance. He was pleased with himself! He was excited about this offer. And well he might be, she acknowledged ruefully. It knocked her approach from Brent Woodford into a cocked hat. 'And they want you to head a new team?'

'That's what he said. Look, Ros, I did intend to discuss it with you before making any final decision. But you know what the last few days were like. We had parties every day, we were out all the time, too shattered to talk at night, and then there were all the arrangements for going down to Hampshire—'

He paused, glanced at her and then said, 'As a matter of fact, I did start to tell you about it. When we were decorating the tree, remember?'

Rosalind opened her mouth and shut it again. Yes, she did remember. He'd wanted to talk to her and she'd stopped him. She hadn't wanted anything serious to mar their Christmas. But—for heaven's sake—how could she have known how serious it was? He ought to have told her. He ought to have insisted she listen.

She took refuge from her guilt in attack. 'All

right, so you never had a chance until you were helping your mother take the turkey out of the oven. But you have a chance now, James. So—discuss.'

He looked at her helplessly. 'Ros, I don't know what to say—'

'Tell me about the job. Tell me what this head-hunter—sounds like someone from a South American jungle!—said to you. Tell me what you told your *mother*, for goodness sake!'

'Well, that's all I did tell her. Not about the head-hunter exactly, but about the job offer. The man she knows is the managing director of IntInt, you see, and when she mentioned him—well, I couldn't help it somehow. It just slipped out that I'd been offered this chance—I was excited about it, Ros.'

'So excited that you managed to keep it to yourself for three whole days before that,' she said bitterly. 'Oh, all right, James, I won't start that again. But I really do think you could have made time ... Or had you made up your mind anyway? Perhaps you weren't thinking of discussing it with me at all? Perhaps you were just looking for a way to *tell* me.'

'No, Ros, I wasn't doing that.' He was beginning to sound angry again. 'Look, I can understand how you feel—I know how I felt when you turned down that offer from Brent Woodford—'

'Do you? But that was different, James, because I did turn it down. You haven't, have you?' She stared at him accusingly. 'You want to accept, don't you? You want to go and work for IntInt—head this wonderful new design team, of which I won't be part—' She stopped suddenly and looked at him, a gleam of hope lighting her dark blue eyes. 'I suppose there isn't a place on this team for me? You weren't thinking of us moving to IntInt together?'

But James shook his head. 'I'm sorry, Ros, no. The team's set up. They were just looking for the leader—and they want me.' He shrugged. 'Look, I haven't made any decision. I wouldn't without talking it over with you first. I just—'

'But you want it all the same. I can tell you do.' She turned away, suddenly blinded by her tears. 'James, I thought we liked being together. I thought we liked sharing our lives. That's why I didn't go to work for Brent—because I wanted to be with you. And now—'

'But I told you, you should have taken that job. It would have been a marvellous chance for you. And if you'd given me the opportunity to talk it over, I'd have urged you to do just that.'

'You don't want us to be together,' she said flatly. 'You don't care if we work in different firms. You—you don't really love me at all.' Her voice was bleak, as bleak as the desolation in her heart. She covered her face with her hands, and then felt James's hand on her shoulder.

'Rosalind, you're talking nonsense. Of course I love you. It's because I love you that I want you to get on, to enjoy your work—to fulfil your potential.' He paused and then added quietly, 'Just as I want to fulfil mine.'

The room was very quiet. From outside, beyond the double glazing, ten floors down, came the low hum of London's traffic. Inside, it was possible to hear the ticking of the carriage clock Rosalind had inherited from her grandmother.

Rosalind lifted her head and looked James straight in the eye. 'You want this job, don't you,' she said. 'You want to take it.'

He nodded. 'Yes. I do. But only if you're happy about it too, Ros.'

'Oh no,' she said, and each word seemed to her to be a knell of doom for their marriage. 'Oh no, James. If you want it, you must take it. Because if you don't, you'll blame me for the rest of your life. You'll always believe I failed you.'

CHAPTER FOUR

The crocuses were out in Hyde Park when James began his new job. Rosalind went there sometimes in her lunch hour and sat on a seat in the early spring sunshine, throwing crumbs to the sparrows and pigeons, and tempting the

65

grey squirrels to come and eat from her hand. The Serpentine lay like a blue jewel under the clear sky and ducks marched busily along its edge, quacking incomprehensible orders to each other.

A year ago, James and I would have been here together, she thought, wandering under trees which were just beginning to burst into leaf. A year ago we had lunch together every day we could, unless one of us had a client or were out of town. A year ago, things were so different...

'But we couldn't go on like that for ever,' James had said when she tried to express her feelings. 'People don't, Ros. It's been great— but we have to go forward. We can't stay stuck in one place all our lives.'

'Why not, if it's a good place to be?' she'd argued, but he shook his head and she knew that his career was beginning to matter more to him than their marriage. More than her. And she turned away, her eyes filling with the tears that seemed to come so easily these days. What had she done wrong? Why was she losing him?

Nothing was the same any more. Their old, easy companionship seemed to have disappeared. They no longer spent their evenings discussing new ideas, designs for a house in the Cotswolds or a flat in Mayfair, matching carpets with curtains or dreaming up excitingly different bathrooms and kitchens. Instead, James took to working in the little room they had set aside as an office, shutting her out. Or, worse still, staying late at IntInt's offices near the Barbican and coming home only when it was time to go to bed.

And did Lisa stay late too? Rosalind wondered, torturing herself with visions of the two of them together. But she dared not ask.

Sighing, she walked slowly back to her own office. And when she reached it, she sat at her desk staring without interest at the plans for the new job she'd been given just that morning—an old cottage in the Cotswolds, not so very far from her mother's home. Someone who had evidently seen and admired some of Rosalind's work. And just the kind of job Rosalind loved.

So why wasn't she feeling more excited? Why wasn't she already visualising the rooms, planning colour schemes, searching through sales catalogues for the antique fittings and furnishings that would go so well together?

'I suppose I'll have to go and see it,' she said to James that evening. 'I can't make any sort of start until I know exactly what it's like.'

'Well, don't get too enthusiastic!' he said with a smile. 'Ros, what's the matter? It's the kind of job you jump at usually. And it's handy for your mother too—why not combine it with a visit to her? You could stay the weekend. You haven't been to stay with her since New Year's Eve.'

'No, I know.' Rosalind remembered the

party Sheila had given then—the perfectly-arranged cottage, the shining glasses, the buffet supper that had taken hours to arrange so meticulously. All her mother's old friends—and the new ones too. The Brigadier, smooth and unctuous, Troy Ballard with his silver eyes and curving smile. 'Well, I suppose we could do that. Perhaps the weekend after next. I can arrange to see the cottage on the Friday or the Monday and we can make a long weekend of it.'

She looked at him expectantly, feeling a stirring of pleasure. A weekend in the country—maybe it was just what they needed. 'You could look at the cottage with me,' she added. 'It would be just like old times...' And then she realised that he was looking uncomfortable, as if he had something to tell her she wasn't going to like. '... James?'

'Ros,' he said, 'I'm sorry, but—I won't be able to come. I've got something to tell you.' She stared at him, her heart suddenly large and heavy in her breast. 'I was going to leave it till later, but—'

'What is it?' She could scarcely get the words out. He's leaving me, she thought, and the world seemed to recede for a moment, then come rushing back so that she put out a hand to steady herself. 'James—what is it?'

'Hey!' He caught at her arm and held her. 'Don't look like that! It's nothing terrible. Here—come and sit down.' He guided her to a

68

chair. 'Ros, you've gone white. What on earth d'you think I'm going to say? It's good news— exciting news.' And she could see now that he was excited, his eyes glowing, his face alight. 'It just means getting through the next few months and then—'

'Then *what*? James, what are you talking about? For God's sake, stop talking in riddles and *tell me*. Why can't you come with me to Mother's? What's happening?'

'All right, all right,' he soothed her. 'Calm down. Nothing awful's going to happen. It just means we're going to be apart a bit more for a few months, but it'll be worth it, I promise you. And when—'

'Apart? What do you mean, apart?'

He took both her hands in his and held them tightly. He looked into her face and she could see the excitement in his, the delight, the pleasure. An excitement, a delight, a pleasure that had nothing to do with her. Her heart was cold now, like a jagged lump of ice. She sat very still, waiting.

'Ros, I saw the MD today. He told me that IntInt are setting up a new branch in Paris. We're really going into Europe, in a big way. There'll be a new design team permanently based there. And he wants me to set it up. Do all the preliminary work. It's to be my baby— mine entirely. What do you think of that?' He was carried away now by his own enthusiasm, hardly seeming to notice Rosalind's frozen expression, the stillness of her body. 'It'll take six months to get it going properly. And I'm to be given a free hand. And I've only been with them for five minutes! Isn't that fantastic?'

Fantastic? Rosalind stared at him. She tried to speak, but so many words were welling up inside her that she hardly knew what to say first. She shook her head, trying to clear it, trying to come to terms with this new idea. '*Paris*?' she whispered at last. 'You never told me you'd be going to Paris!'

'I didn't know, when the job started. I just told you, it's a new opening, and it's been brought forward. Ros, you knew my work was going to involve quite a bit of travelling—'

'Travelling, yes.' And it had taken her quite a while to come to terms with that, she thought—if indeed she had come to terms with it at all. She still didn't like spending her evenings and nights alone in the flat while James was away on one of the big projects IntInt seemed to concentrate on. 'But six months living in France isn't exactly what I'd call travelling.'

'Well, it may not be that long. It depends how difficult it is to set up the new branch. And it isn't exactly "six months living in France," Ros. Paris is no more than a hop, skip and jump away these days. I can be home on Friday evenings almost as quickly as I am now. I'll only be away four nights a week—'

'You mean you'll only be home *three* nights
70

a week. It depends how you look at it, doesn't it. And I suppose the glamorous Lisa will be going with you too.'

'She is my secretary,' he said briefly.

'And she did get to move with you when you went to work for IntInt, I know. Lucky Lisa. It was more than you could arrange for your wife, wasn't it—but then I suppose it depends what—or who—is most important to you.'

Rosalind heard her words with horror, but there seemed to be nothing she could do to stop them. They poured out, and she heard herself saying things that appalled her, things she had never thought to hear herself saying to James, her James, the man she loved and had married and wanted to spend all her life with. 'Why are you doing this to me?' she demanded bitterly. 'You know I turned down a good job just because I wanted to be with you. Why don't you want to be with me?'

She turned away from him, feeling the sick sensation of rejection, the certainty that James no longer loved her. 'It's Lisa, isn't it? Oh, don't pretend any more. Why else would you have taken her with you to IntInt? Why else should she be going to Paris with you?'

Her voice rose as she swung back, accusing him with her voice, her eyes, every taut line of her slender body. 'Just what will you be doing in Paris, the two of you? Working side by side all day ... and in the evenings—what then?'

James stared at her. She saw his eyes darken

and narrow, as they did when he was really angry. For a moment, she was afraid. She wished she could call back the words, blot out the feeling behind them. But it couldn't be done. It was there, the dread of losing him, the fear, the jealousy, sweeping her along. And the words had been said.

'Just what are you implying, Rosalind?'

Really scared now, she tried to backtrack, to cover her words with a laugh, to turn them into a joke.

'Implying? I'm not implying anything, James—what's happened to your sense of humour? You seem to take things so seriously these days.'

'No,' he said, and reached out to lay one hand on her shoulder. 'No, I haven't lost my sense of humour, Ros. And I still know when you're joking. You meant what you said just now and I want to know just what you're implying. Are you seriously suggesting there's something going on between me and Lisa?'

Rosalind met his eyes. His hand felt heavy on her shoulder, the fingers tight. She saw the anger in his face, felt her own misery sweep over her.

'You tell me,' she said, and heard the note of desolation in her voice. 'You tell me if anything's going on, James. Because I'm not going to know, am I? I hardly ever see you these days. Oh—' her voice broke and she turned away, '—what's happened to us?

Everything was all right until you took this job. We were happy. We shared everything—our lives, our work, all of it. Now—now I never see you during the day and you're often away at night as well. And now you're talking about going to Paris for six months. Paris! With *Lisa!*'

'I'm talking about my job,' he said tautly. 'My career. My life.'

'And mine! It's my life too!'

'Yes, it's your life too. And if you remember, when you had a similar opportunity I wanted you to take it—'

'But I didn't want to! I didn't want to leave you—'

'Rosalind, get this straight. *I am not leaving you.* All I'm doing is setting up a new branch in Paris, which will take me six months, during which time I shall be away five days—four nights—a week. And after that—'

'Yes?' she said bitterly. 'After that? Tell me what will happen after that, James.'

He hesitated. 'Ros, it's difficult—'

'You bet it's difficult!' she flashed. 'Because it's not something you can tell me easily, is it! But I'm not a fool, James. I can see the writing on the wall. This is the beginning, isn't it? The beginning of the end.'

She jumped up and began to walk about the room, twisting her hands together, misery and pain surging inside her. 'Six months in Paris with Lisa ... it's perfectly obvious what will happen. You don't *have* to tell me.'

James sat quite still. He looked almost as if he had been struck. Rosalind felt a moment of fear. Had she gone too far? How could she have said such things? She didn't really suspect James of planning an affair with his secretary. But something deep inside had driven her on, forced the words from her mouth, and she hadn't been able to suppress them.

'Rosalind,' he said at last, and his voice was very quiet, as if he dared not let it rise. 'Rosalind, let's stop this. We're both going to say things we'll regret, things we'll never be able to put out of our minds. You don't really believe what you've been saying. You don't really believe there could be anything between me and Lisa.'

Rosalind stared at him. Then she sat down in a big armchair, perching herself on the edge, her hands clasped tightly together on her knees. 'I don't know what I believe any more, James,' she said huskily. 'You're away so much—and when you're home I feel we're strangers. We don't seem to communicate any more. I—I don't know what's happening to us. I feel—frightened.'

He looked at her, then reached across and laid his hands gently on hers. 'But there's nothing to be frightened of, Ros. I'm just going to be away for part of the time—not much more than half of it—for a few months. That's all there is to it. Millions of people have to work away from home. Sailors—soldiers—oilmen—all kinds of people. They survive, and so do their wives. Six months isn't the end of the world, now is it?'

She gazed down at her hands, hardly able to see them through her tears, and shook her head.

'It'll be gone in no time. You'll have plenty to do—you've got your own work. And when it's over, we'll plan a holiday, a really good one. Somewhere you've always wanted to go. The Seychelles, perhaps, or the Caribbean. How does that sound?'

'Wonderful,' Rosalind said, but there was no enthusiasm in her voice. The Caribbean? The Seychelles? But suppose she and James weren't even together by that time. Suppose—just suppose he and Lisa...

Six months in Paris, with a beautiful secretary. And nothing Rosalind could do about it. No way she could stop the inevitable happening.

'Better now?' James asked, and she felt a sudden surge of anger. He was talking to her as if she were a child! Soothing her, offering her sweets if she was a good girl. *Patronising* her!

I won't be patronised, she thought furiously. I won't be treated like a little girl who's run to mummy to be kissed better. I'm a woman, and I can take care of myself. I won't sit at home like a parcel, waiting to be claimed when he chooses to come back and be my husband

75

again. And I won't let him see how I feel about it any more.

She lifted her head and looked him straight in the eye. Like hell she'd let him see her cry over this again. Like hell he'd see how scared and miserable and jealous she felt. 'Yes, thank you,' she said coolly. 'Much better. And I agree—the time will just fly by. As you say, I'll have plenty to do.'

And before her tears could betray her again, she stood up and walked, straight-backed, out of the living room and into the bedroom, and closed the door quietly but firmly behind her.

But once inside, the misery surged over her again and she leaned against the door, fighting her tears. The clean, sparse whiteness of the room, which had pleased her so much when she and James had designed it, was suddenly stark and cold. And she wondered how she was ever going to get through so many lonely nights here, when James was in Paris with Lisa.

*　　*　　*

'Darling, it's lovely to see you again. It's been ages.' Sheila drew Rosalind into the cottage, hugged her and then held her at arm's length to inspect her. 'And looking so gorgeous, too! But haven't you lost weight?'

'A little. And I think I needed to.' Rosalind slid out of her jacket and gave it to her mother to hang up. She went into the sitting room and

76

crossed to the window. 'The garden's looking lovely.'

'Yes, it's always at its best with the spring flowers. Now, what are you going to have to drink? Gin? Martini?' Sheila busied herself at the small side table. 'And tell me about James and this wonderful new job of his. I suppose you'll be flying off to Paris at weekends to be with him? So exciting!'

Flying to Paris? Rosalind took her drink and looked at it as if it could tell her something. James had never once suggested her going to him in Paris—all his talk had been about his coming back to London. And not even that, sometimes. Some weekends—like this one— would be just too busy to spare any time at all.

'No, I don't think I'll be doing that,' she said at last. 'I'm busy too, you know. I've got several new projects on hand at present and they're going to take up all my time. Like this cottage at Over Hathersleigh. Weekends are really the only time the owner can spare to talk to me.'

'Oh yes, you mentioned that on the phone. It's that beautiful little thatched cottage on the edge of the village, isn't it? It's being restored— neglected for years but now the old woman's died her children have sold it. I'm so glad Troy's asked you to do the interior. He was obviously impressed by—'

'*Troy?*' Rosalind broke in. 'You mean Troy Ballard? It's *his* cottage?'

'Well, of course it is. Surely you knew that.' Sheila gave her a surprised glance. 'What's the matter, Rosalind? It doesn't make any difference, does it?'

'No—no, of course not.' Hastily, Rosalind pulled herself together. 'I just hadn't realised, that's all. I thought he'd bought Stret Barn.'

'No, that purchase fell through and then this lovely old cottage came on the market and he snapped it up instead. I thought I'd told you.' Sheila gave her a look of total innocence. 'Naturally, he asked me if I thought you would do the interior. I told him to apply to the firm, of course—I knew you'd hate me to influence him in any way. But I was sure you knew the job was for him.'

'No—no, I didn't. I haven't really looked at the papers at all,' Rosalind confessed. 'I just picked the file up and put it in my briefcase. I was going to look at it this evening.'

'Well, Troy's coming round later for coffee, so it's just as well you found out.' Sheila spoke disapprovingly, as if she thought Rosalind had been slack in not giving her work more thought beforehand.

But there really wasn't anything I could do before I actually see the cottage, she defended herself.

All the same, it could have been very embarrassing if Troy had arrived and she had had no idea it was his cottage she was to work on.

'I'd better look at the papers now,' she said, getting to her feet. 'And I'll take my case up and unpack as well. Dinner at the usual time?'

'In half an hour. And Troy's coming at eight-thirty, so put on something pretty.' Sheila gave her another little hug as she went towards the kitchen. 'It *is* so nice to have you here, and all to myself too. Not that I'm not *very* fond of dear James, but you know what I mean—we can be cosy on our own, can't we? Just girls together.'

But we're not girls together, Rosalind thought as she carried her case up to her room. We're mother and daughter. And she felt again the familiar suffocation, followed as always by the same old guilt. Poor Mother—she only had Rosalind, after all. No wonder she looked forward to these visits; no wonder she went a bit over the top with her welcome. And maybe Rosalind had shut her out a bit since she and James got married...

Well, I'll have time to make up for it now, she thought wryly. I can come down for weekends—have Mother up at the flat too, take her to a show and out to dinner. She'll love that. And we can have long, girlish talks late into the night.

Meanwhile, she'd better do as Sheila had suggested and look at the papers she'd been given about Troy's cottage. And have a shower and change her clothes.

Put on something pretty, Sheila had said—

almost as if Troy were her 'date'. He wasn't, of course—but all the same, at the memory of those silver eyes and that enigmatic, appreciative smile, Rosalind was conscious of a small quickening of excitement. Maybe the weekend was going to be more interesting than she'd thought.

*　　*　　*

'Well, this is it.' Troy came round to open the passenger door and Rosalind climbed out and stood for a moment gazing at the cottage, half-hidden behind its shaggy hedge.

The garden was overgrown and strewn with builders' paraphernalia—ladders, a cement mixer, piles of rubble and a stack of new bricks. But in the midst of all this debris, the cottage stood as it had stood for three centuries, firm and solid, as if it had grown out of the ground.

'Looks a bit of a mess at present,' he observed, going through the gap where once, presumably, a gate had hung. 'But they assure me it'll all come straight eventually. I thought it'd be a good idea to get you in on things at this stage though, rather than wait until later. You might have some better ideas than the architect has had.'

'Oh, I hardly think so.' Rosalind followed him, still gazing at the cottage with its timber framing, its thatched roof and leaded windows.

She stopped for a moment, assessing its proportions. 'Troy, it's a gem.'

'Well, I thought so.' He smiled down at her. 'I see we think alike about these things. And I know I'm going to love your ideas about how to do the interior.'

He produced a key and opened the front door. Rosalind found herself in a large room, the walls of rough stone and the floors scattered with tools, wood and buckets. She gazed around.

'Can you see it ever being a home again?' Troy was beside her, a note of rueful amusement in his voice. 'See, they've knocked down all the interior walls here—this part used to be two small rooms and a tiny hall. Gerry— the architect, he's a friend of mine—said it would be better opened out and I agree with him. Had to put in a couple of RSJ's of course, to replace the supporting walls, but that seems to have worked OK. So I'll have one big living room—with the inglenook fireplace over here—and a good-sized kitchen, I'll show you that in a minute, and this small room here's been left as my study. I like to have that on the ground floor. There's to be a small cloakroom here, and three bedrooms and a bathroom upstairs.'

As he talked, he prowled around, gesturing with his long, tapering hands. Then he stopped and gave Rosalind a smile. 'Well? Think you'll be able to do something spectacular with this

81

rather unpromising raw material?'

'Unpromising? I think it's fabulous!' Rosalind moved quickly about, assessing the room from different angles, looking out of the windows, peeping in at the rooms designated for study and cloakroom. 'And this is the kitchen? Why, it's marvellous, a really good size. I can do a lot of things with a kitchen like this. Can I go upstairs?' She was half-way up them already. 'Oh yes, I like this. Lovely deep windowsills. And you know, there's room for an *en suite* bathroom in this biggest room. Didn't your architect friend suggest that?'

'Yes, he did, but I hadn't decided finally. You think it's a good idea?'

'Oh yes. Everyone wants an *en suite* bathroom these days. Yes, it has a lot of potential.' Rosalind leaned from the window. 'The garden's quite big actually, isn't it? Are you having it landscaped?'

'I will later, when the builders have done their worst.' He joined her at the window and they gazed out together. 'Nice view, isn't it? Hardly a man-made artefact in sight.'

'There isn't, is there?' She was conscious of him standing close to her, of the warmth of his body, the slightly musky tones of his aftershave. Suddenly, she could think of nothing to say. Casting wildly for inspiration, she said, 'Are you going to be living here? All the time, I mean?'

'Most of it, yes. I have to go away

sometimes, on business, but this will be my main base. It's ideal for me—quiet, yet convenient for London. And I can do a lot of my business from home.'

'I see.' Rosalind was a little uncertain as to what Troy's business actually was. Importing, and that sort of thing, he'd said vaguely when they'be been chatting the evening before. But Sheila hadn't really allowed much private conversation. She'd welcomed Troy almost as if he'd come specially to see her, and had held his attention during the entire visit, keeping up an endless flow of bright chatter. Not that she'd excluded Rosalind—on the contrary, she had brought her daughter's name and accomplishments into almost every sentence. But she'd given Rosalind very little chance to speak for herself.

'I'm glad to have this chance of being on our own,' Troy said suddenly, and she blushed as if he'd been reading her thoughts. 'I've been wanting to talk to you ever since we met before Christmas.'

'About the cottage?' she smiled, and he shook his head.

'Not about the cottage! About you. I find you very ... interesting.' He half-turned towards her, leaning back against the wall, and Rosalind was aware of his magnetism. She moved slightly away and looked out at the view of rolling Cotswold hills. The trees in the garden were coming into leaf—slightly later than those in London, she thought detachedly.

Without looking at him, she said lightly, 'Oh, I'm not very interesting, I'm afraid. Just an ordinary working girl.'

'Not ordinary at all. And not just a "working girl" either, surely. You hold down quite a high-powered job.'

'Not as high-powered as it could be,' she said without thinking, and found herself telling him all about the job Brent Woodford had offered her. 'It would have been quite a step up for me, but I didn't take it because—well, James and I have always worked together. I wouldn't have dreamed of moving on without him.'

'But surely you're not working together now?' Troy asked. 'You were telling me last night—your mother was—that he's doing some project in Paris at the moment. Why aren't you over there with him?'

'Oh, James was head-hunted.' She spoke as if it couldn't matter less. 'He was offered this fabulous job setting up a new branch for IntInt—I daresay you've heard of them. Much too good to turn down, of course, so off he went.'

'And you didn't go with him?'

'I wasn't invited.'

There was a short silence. Rosalind was aware of him, standing there, still quite close to her. She turned her head slowly and found him watching her, his eyes dark as pewter.

'It hurts, doesn't it,' he said gently, and she

felt the tears hot in her eyes.

'I'm sorry—I don't—'

'It's all right.' Troy reached out and touched her hand. 'You don't have to say anything. I didn't mean to pry.'

'You're not—it's just—oh, this is silly.' She fumbled for a handkerchief. 'Look, there isn't anything wrong between James and me, please don't think that. We're—we're very happy together. It's just that I—well, I miss him and—'

'Of course.' Troy's hand was under her elbow. She could feel the shape of his fingers through her sleeve. Long fingers, musician's fingers, sensitive fingers. 'It must be very disappointing for you. Especially when you've turned down your own chance.'

'Yes.' She looked up at him, grateful for his understanding. 'Yes, it is. You see, I *like* working with James. And I thought—I thought—' The tears threatened again and she turned away, but Troy held her, drawing her closer. She felt a sudden strong desire to lay her head on his shoulder and weep in earnest.

'You thought he liked working with you. And I'm sure he did; he'd be mad not to. But you're contending with the male ego, you see.' Troy laughed, a little self-deprecatingly. 'I'm afraid we all have it. The desire to get on—shine at something. Achieve. The temptation was obviously just too great.'

'I can never win, then, can I?' Rosalind said

85

disheartened.

'Never win? But of course you can!' He gave her shoulders a squeeze. 'Rosalind, you've already had one good offer. That wasn't the only one in the world. You'll have others, even better. You can outstrip that husband of yours any day of the week, just wait and see! IntInt? They're not the only firm going into Europe. Why, you've hardly begun.'

Rosalind looked up at him. 'You really think so?'

'I know so,' he said firmly. 'Now—let's have a look at those plans and start getting some ideas together. I want to hear just what you think I ought to have in my fantastic, exotic master bedroom.' He grinned with a touch of wickedness. 'Apart from a fantastic, exotic mistress, of course—though if you've any suggestions to make in that direction I'll be only too glad to hear them...'

Rosalind laughed and began to feel better. She moved away from the window and picked up her briefcase. She took out the architect's plans and spread them on the wide windowsill.

'You know, you're very good for me,' she said to Troy as they pored over the sheet together. 'You make me believe I could actually go places.'

'But of course you can go places,' he told her, and once again she was conscious of his shoulder, pressed lightly but warmly against hers. 'Any place you like. The sky's the limit for you, Rosalind. You've got talent and you've got guts. I know—I've seen it before, that special quality.'

She turned her head in surprise and found his face close to hers, his breath warm on her cheek, his lips almost touching her hair. 'A very special quality,' he said quietly, and they both stayed quite still, as if to move would be to set off a reaction that could not be revoked.

Rosalind held her breath. Her heart was jumping raggedly, her skin tingling. She felt her lips part and knew she should move away, but her limbs seemed to have lost their power.

Then Troy smiled and shifted his stance. The movement took him slightly away from her, so that they were not so electrifyingly close, and Rosalind found she could breathe again. She turned, fumbled with the plans, wished her hands would stop shaking, and heard Troy speak from the other side of the room.

'Come and look at this, Rosalind. It must have been a cupboard, set in the thickness of the wall. I'd like to make a feature of it—what do you think?'

Almost weak with relief, she folded the plans and went across. Together they examined the cupboard, then moved about the rooms considering what might be done with them and how they might be decorated. Gradually, Rosalind forgot those few moments when she had been so aware of his virile allure, when she had been ready to go into his arms and weep out all her unhappiness. By the time they left the cottage, they were laughing and talking with the easy familiarity of old friends.

But those moments were not entirely forgotten. And as Troy locked the door behind them, he paused, then looked down at Rosalind, and his eyes were grave, 'Look—it may not be my place to say this, Rosalind. I'm sure you've got a lot of friends you can turn to. And there's your mother too. But—well, if ever you need anyone to talk to—about anything, you know—well, you can always call on me. Any time. And I mean that. I'd be only too pleased to help if you thought I could.'

Rosalind looked at him and smiled. 'Thank you, Troy. I'll remember that.'

And before she realised quite what she was doing, she reached up and drew his head down to hers, and kissed him.

CHAPTER FIVE

'... and so we've taken on this enormous project,' James finished, closing the folder and leaning back in his chair. 'A *chateau*, no less! What d'you think of that?'

'Marvellous,' Rosalind said. She reached across and took the folder, flipping it open to look at the plans, the sketches James had made of some of the rooms and his ideas for their decoration. How she would have loved to work on this with him, she thought sadly. To share in his excitement, visiting the *chateau*, considering the rooms, visualising them with just the right kind of furniture, the fabrics and carpeting that would bring them to life. But it was nothing to do with her now. She was only a spectator, applauding from the sidelines.

'Of course, it's not a big *chateau*,' James said with an attempt at nonchalance. 'Really not much more than a large country house. But it's got real atmosphere and a character all its own. I'd like you to see it, Ros.'

'Yes, I'd like to see it too,' she said politely, and laid the folder on the coffee table between them.

'No, I really mean I *want* you to see it.' James reached out and touched the folder, as if he couldn't quite bear to let it out of his hands. 'I'd like to hear your ideas—you'd be bound to have lots, things I wouldn't think of. You could—'

'But you forget.' Rosalind felt a spurt of anger. 'I don't work for IntInt, James. It's your job, not mine.'

He looked at her in surprise. 'I know that, but I'd have thought you'd be interested.'

'Interested, yes.' She heard the hard edge to her voice and felt some surprise. 'But my time doesn't come cheap, James. If you want to employ me as a consultant—'

'Ros, that's silly!'

'Is it? Why?'

'Well, because I'm not asking you in that sort of capacity at all. I just want you to see it, enjoy it with me, and if you have any ideas I'd be pleased to consider them.'

'Very kind of you,' Rosalind said coldly. She got up and walked away, towards the kitchen. 'But in my book, that's *consultancy*, James. Remember how you used to feel when people we hardly knew tried to get us to give them ideas on their own houses, for nothing, just because they'd asked us to a party? Or met us at someone else's party? No, if you want my ideas you'll have to pay for them. In fact, you ought really to pay Lords & Ladies for my time. I think that's what you used to tell those people, wasn't it?'

James looked at her. His face was closed and angry. He said, 'You're making altogether too much of this, Ros. I told you, I just want you to enjoy it with me.'

Rosalind had reached the kitchen door. She stopped and looked back at him. 'The only way I could enjoy it with you, James,' she said clearly, 'would be to work on it with you. Properly. As a colleague. As—as we used to be.'

To her fury, her voice trembled and broke on the last words and she turned and walked blindly through the door into the kitchen. She leaned against the sink, fighting to control the tears that had so unexpectedly threatened.

Why did she always have to be so emotional? she thought angrily. Why couldn't she stay calm and rational? But it wasn't a rational situation. The whole idea of James splitting their life by going to work for a different firm, and then making it even worse by going to France for six months, *was* an emotional one. And it did upset her—how could she even try to pretend otherwise?

The door opened and James came into the kitchen. He stood for a moment looking at her and she thought how attractive he was with his thick black hair and dark, velvet-brown eyes. He was wearing casual clothes tonight—dark slacks and a sweater so brightly-coloured that it would have turned heads on a ski slope. His lean, rangy figure moved with a grace few men seemed to accomplish, so that people often took him for an actor or dancer. Rosalind had even seen girls in restaurants eyeing him and then whispering together, clearly trying to decide if he was someone they'd seen in a film or on stage. Once one of the bolder ones had approached him and asked for his autograph.

And he looked like this in Paris, every day when he was with his secretary, Lisa. He looked as attractive and dangerous and downright *sexy* when they were working together. Or meeting in the evening for a drink, or dinner.

Did they do that? Did they meet in the evenings? He'd never admitted it, but it would be stupid to imagine they didn't. Two English people, alone together in Paris ... Of course they met, and had dinner, perhaps danced a little. And then...?

Tormented by her thoughts, Rosalind turned her head away. James came across the small, white kitchen and tried to draw her into his arms. 'Ros,' he said gently, 'please don't get so upset. There really isn't any need.'

'Isn't there?' she said, stubbornly resisting him and keeping her face averted. 'Maybe you don't see it quite the way I do.'

'Well, no, I don't think I do.' He dropped his hands from her shoulders. 'You see, I never thought there was anything to make a fuss about in the first place. We liked our job and we liked working together, but we both knew it couldn't last—'

'We didn't! *I* didn't. And why couldn't it? If we liked sharing our work—our *lives*—why couldn't we go on doing it? You didn't have to go and work for IntInt.'

James sighed. 'I know I didn't have to. But surely we both wanted to get on. We don't want to stay in the same place for ever, do we?'

'I don't see why not,' Rosalind muttered, 'if it's a place we both like.'

James looked at her for a moment. 'Well, we'll have to agree to differ on that, I'm afraid. Because much as I liked working for Lords & Ladies, it wasn't my ambition to stay there for ever. I didn't think it was yours either.'

'So maybe you should have asked me,' she said angrily. 'Maybe you shouldn't have just made assumptions about me.'

'And maybe you shouldn't have made them about me!' he retorted, and then laid his hands on her shoulders again. 'Ros, listen. I don't want to shut myself away from you. That's why I want to share this job with you—I want you to come and see the *chateau* with me, so that we can talk about it together. So that you can enjoy it too.'

'I see. You want me to come over to France, spend the weekend looking at this glorified country house, give you my ideas—and then come back again and slip back into my own little rut, the rut that's too dull for you to spend your life in. While you do all the exciting work with Lisa. While you really share your life with her.' Ros flung him a bitter glance. 'D'you know how that strikes me? As crumbs from the rich man's table—that's how! And my answer to that is—thanks, but no thanks.'

James was silent. His dark eyes moved slowly over her face. He shook his head. 'You really are determined so see this all your own way, aren't you, Ros?'

'And aren't you doing just the same?' she flung at him. 'Have you given any thought at all to how I feel?'

'Yes, as a matter of fact, I have.' He was losing patience, she realised, and she felt a sudden quiver of perverse pleasure at having

93

stung him at last. It was no fun being the only emotional one, after all. It would be good for James to lose that calm, rational exterior and let his real feelings show—yet even as she thought this, so fleetingly she was scarcely aware of the thought, she felt a tremor of apprehension. Did she really *want* to know what James thought and felt about her? Could she cope with the knowledge?

'I've thought quite a lot about how you feel,' James went on quietly. 'And do you want to know what I think?'

She lifted her head, meeting his eyes, determined not to let him know how she was feeling now. How could he pretend to understand her anyway?

'I think you're jealous,' he said, and Rosalind gasped. 'Jealous of the fact that I've got this job, and—worse than that—jealous of Lisa because she's in Paris too. You know what your trouble is? You're so insecure, you're frightened to let me out of your sight. That's why you want us to work together—so that you know where I am and who I'm with every minute of the day. You can't bear to think I might be doing something you've no share in, you can't bear to think I might be with another woman, even if we're only working together. In fact, you can't bear to think I might let a minute go by without thinking about *you*. You want to be there all the time, beside me, behind me, around me, in my head!'

He dropped his hands and turned away, running one hand through his hair from forehead to nape, like a man in the throes of despair. 'My God, Rosalind, don't you realise what it's doing to us, this insane possessiveness of yours? Don't you see that it'll drive us apart in the end, if you don't get hold of it? Can't you understand at *all*?'

There was a deathly silence in the kitchen. Rosalind clutched the edge of the sink as if it were the only stability in the entire universe. Without it, she might have gone spinning into space, never to be caught and brought back to earth.

'*Jealous?*' she whispered at last. '*Possessive?* I don't know how you can say those things to me. I just love you. That's all.' Once again, her voice broke and she felt the tears begin to stream down her face. 'I love you, James.'

Her hands were clamped tightly to the edge of the sink. She unhooked them, painfully, and brought them up to her cheeks. The tears dripped through her fingers. Oh, why did she have to *cry*?

James turned back to her. He came close and drew her into his arms, and this time she didn't resist.

'Oh, James,' she whispered, and laid her head against his chest.

'Ros, listen to me,' he said when the storm had subsided a little. 'I know you love me. I've never doubted it. And I love you. You must believe that.' He paused for a moment and she sniffed and blew her nose, giving him a shaky smile before laying her head against him again. 'But even if people love each other as much as we do, they can't live in each other's pockets all the time. They have to have some time to be individuals—to be themselves.'

'But we *are* individuals. I'm independent—I lived for years on my own before we got married. And I've always loved your individuality.' She stroked the bright sweater. 'I've never wanted to tie you down, James. But we work so well together—I can't see why it has to be broken up.'

'Maybe that *is* why,' he said slowly. 'We do work well together, Ros. I can't deny that—I don't want to. But maybe we have to separate for a while to let ourselves develop in our own ways, rather than as a couple. Don't you think—'

'*Separate?*' she broke in, her eyes wide. 'James, what are you saying? Surely you don't—'

'I don't mean it in that way, of course I don't. Just as far as our work's concerned. Look, it doesn't have to be for ever, Ros. One day, maybe there'll be a vacancy at IntInt and—'

'And you can put in a word for me,' she said scornfully, pulling away from him. 'No thank you, James. I told you—I don't want crumbs from the rich man's table. If you're so keen on us both developing our individuality, that's what I'll do. And the next good job that comes along, I'll take. Maybe I'll even go back to Brent Woodford and ask him if his offer is still open.'

She threw him a defiant glance but he stayed silent, watching her with dark, unreadable eyes. 'Or maybe I'll do something quite different,' she went on recklessly. 'Something entirely on my own. How would you like that, James?'

'So long as it was something that you really wanted to do and it made you happy, I wouldn't mind at all,' he said quietly. 'But don't just rush off and do something in an effort to score points, Ros. That won't help either of us. It'll only make things worse.'

'And that's just how you'd see it, isn't it! As an effort to score points. Not as an effort to develop my own individuality—wasn't that how you put it? *That* only applies when it's you who are taking off and doing what you like.'

'Ros, I've told you—'

'Oh, I know what you've told me,' she declared. 'You put it so clearly. And so reasonably. I only wish I were a man too, so that I could be as clear and rational and—and sensible about it all. But unfortunately, I'm not. I'm just a stupid, emotional woman. And possessive and jealous into the bargain. No wonder you'd rather spend your time in Paris with Lisa!'

There was a long silence. After a few moments, she moved away and began to look in the freezer, fiddling with packets of frozen peas and unappetising pieces of fish.

James rested against the kitchen table, watching her. At last he stood up. 'There's not much more I can say, is there?' His voice was even. 'You seem determined that there's something going on between me and Lisa— you keep coming back to that, like a dog digging up a bone. And nothing I can say is going to change your mind, is it?'

He waited for a moment, but Rosalind said nothing. She began to pull things out of the freezer and pile them up on the worktop, as if searching for some long-lost treasure. 'All right,' he said at last, 'I get the message. You don't want to talk any more now. But we can't let it go at that, Rosalind. We have to talk sometime. We have to sort this out, or it's going to cause trouble again. And we may never get rid of it.'

He turned and walked out of the kitchen. A few minutes later, Rosalind heard the front door open and close, and knew that he had gone out.

She left the frozen foods piled on the table and sank into a chair. She rested her head on her hands and let the emotion, the frustration and the despair wash over her in a great tidal flood. And this time, when the tears came, she made no attempt to hold them back. She laid her arms on the table and bent her head down to them and wept.

She wept for all the loving that she and James had shared, for the closeness she had believed to exist between them. For the joy, the laughter, the delight, the sheer full-blooded happiness.

She wept for it all. For all that they seemed to have lost.

*   *   *

'So James is staying in Paris again this weekend?' Sheila's voice was just not quite casual enough.

Rosalind turned away, fiddling with her bag as if looking for something. She found a handkerchief, took it out, dabbed at her lips before answering. 'Mm. A special assignment.' Goodness, she was making him sound like a second-rate spy! 'IntInt have been asked to decorate a restored *chateau*. Only a small one, but it's quite exciting. They hadn't actually intended taking on any real projects yet, not until the new branch is properly under way, but the owner's English apparently and has seen some of James's work and asked for him specially, so . . .' She became aware that she was talking too fast and let her voice trail away.

Sheila was watching her speculatively and she had a nasty feeling that her mother wasn't fooled in the slightest.

'How thrilling. I suppose that's where they'll get a lot of their Continental business—from English people settling over there. Now that we're really integrated into the Community, and especially with property so cheap in France, there must be a lot of people thinking of moving. I wonder you and James don't consider it yourselves.'

'Going to live in France?' Rosalind was startled. 'It's never even crossed my mind.'

'But wouldn't you like to do it? Something completely different—new, exciting.' Sheila's voice was animated. 'And now's the time, when you're young and energetic and don't have any responsibilities. I'm sure it must have occurred to James.'

'No!' Rosalind was surprised by her own vehemence. 'He hasn't—I'd know. And he doesn't want to move any more than I do. This is just for six months, no more. He'll be as pleased as I will when it's over and he's based in London again.'

'Will he?' Sheila's face was thoughtful. 'I wonder ... Still, you're probably right. You know him a lot better than I do. And the time will soon be up, won't it? We keep talking about six months but it's less than five now. And there's one good thing about it.' She leaned forward and gave Rosalind's arm a little pat. 'It gives us some time to be together, doesn't it? I told you last time you came, I'm really *very* fond of James, but it is nice to have you to myself occasionally. And I'm going to make the most of these little visits of yours.'

Rosalind looked at her mother and smiled, a little uncertainly. She still wasn't sure that she was doing the right thing in coming down to stay with her mother whenever James was away for the weekend.

But the flat in London seemed so empty without him, the time from Friday evening until Monday morning a desert of loneliness. And here in the perfect little cottage behind Sheila's small antique shop, she could revert a little to the child she had once been. She could wallow in the feeling that someone would take care of her.

I need someone to take care of me, she thought sadly, as Sheila fetched a drink and set it on the table beside her. I get tired of being independent all the time.

But it wasn't really her mother she wanted to take care of her. It was James.

And James was in Paris. With Lisa.

'Oh, by the way.' Sheila's voice broke the silence. 'I've asked Richard to dinner this evening. I hope you don't mind. We'll have plenty of time to be on our own over the rest of the weekend. You remember Richard, don't you?'

'Richard? Oh yes—the Brigadier.' Rosalind felt a faint irritation. Why did her mother have to do this, producing guests as if she felt that Rosalind needed to be entertained every time

101

she visited? Didn't she realise that her daughter would be perfectly happy sitting by the fire with a book, watching TV or even indulging in one of the 'girls' chats' that Sheila talked about but never seemed actually to have time for? Last time it had been Troy Ballard ... Her heart quickened a little at the memory of that visit to his cottage. And she'd be seeing him again tomorrow, she thought, to talk over the ideas she'd drawn up. A faint flush warmed her cheeks and she became guiltily aware that her mother was speaking again.

'Really, Rosalind, you're in a world of your own these days. I was telling you, the Brigadier has been helping me find stock for the shop. He brought in some very nice porcelain the other day, early Wedgwood. And last week he took me to a house sale over the other side of Stratford and we bought some good furniture—small pieces, you know I don't have room for anything very large. He seems to have quite an eye for it.'

'That's good.' Rosalind's response was mechanical. She really wasn't very interested in the Brigadier—she hadn't like him all that much, pleasant though he'd been. Almost ingratiation, she'd thought ... She remembered James's speculations about her mother and the Brigadier, but dismissed the thought at once. That was nonsense. As if her mother would be interested in that sort of thing, at her age!

All the same, she couldn't help noticing that the Brigadier seemed very much at home in the little cottage, helping Sheila to fetch new courses and putting fresh logs on the fire. And he treated Rosalind as if she were a person of considerable importance, asking diligently after James and her life in London, inquiring about her job—though she had a feeling he didn't really approve of young married women having careers, and thought she ought to spend her time at home, preparing meals for the lord and master and perhaps knitting him sweaters in her spare time.

She was half amused and half repelled by this show of old-world charm. Buttering me up, she thought cynically, trying to get me on his side. Mother might not be interested in him, but he's certainly interested in her.

Or maybe it would be more true to say that he was interested in her antique shop . . .

He left at last and Sheila came back, having taken what Rosalind thought a ridiculously long time to show him out, and sank down into an armchair.

She kicked off her shoes and stretched her feet out to the fire, wriggling her toes. 'Mm, that's better ... I've sometimes thought of suggesting to Richard that he bring his own slippers, simply so that I could wear mine. But I don't know ... it seems just a touch too domestic.' She slanted a look at Rosalind. 'What do you think?'

Rosalind shrugged. 'It's up to you.' In spite of the Brigadier's attention, she felt somehow disgruntled by the evening, as if she'd been left out of something. Perhaps it was because she felt that his attention, although apparently focused on herself, had really been directed at Sheila. As if he wanted Sheila to see how well he could get along with her daughter. How well he would fit into the family...

Oh, stop it, she told herself crossly. There's no possibility whatsoever that he and Mother ... But all the same, she couldn't help feeling that tiny niggle of anxiety. And it was coupled with resentment. After all, she hadn't come down here this weekend to play gooseberry to a couple of people who were too old to be thinking of that kind of thing. She'd come for a little bit of cossetting on her own account. She was miserable, for heaven's sake. She needed some comfort.

'So you're seeing Troy tomorrow?' Sheila spoke casually, without looking at her.

'Yes. I'm going over to the house he's renting and we're going to look at the ideas I've sketched out, and then we're going to the cottage. We'll probably have lunch in a pub somewhere.'

'Bring him back to tea if you like. Or dinner, if you're going to be later.'

'I might.' Rosalind's voice was equally casual. Of course there was nothing between her and Troy, despite that brief kiss at his cottage gate the other week. But he was an attractive man and good company—and if James was going to be enjoying himself in Paris, there was no reason on earth why she shouldn't pass her own time as pleasantly as possible. Anyway, it was as much business as pleasure. The task of refurbishing Troy's cottage was a plum job and one she really intended to make a success of. She was already thinking of trying to interest one of the major glossy magazines in it.

She mentioned this idea to Troy as he brought a tray of coffee into his sitting room next morning. The house he was renting was an Edwardian villa which stood on the edge of the village, looking rather out of place amongst the Cotswold houses that surrounded it, and he'd already apologised rather wryly for the decor.

'Don't take this as an example of my taste,' he'd begged her as she came through the front door. 'I don't want to find you've designed a replica of suburban Thirties nastiness, flying ducks and all!'

'Flying ducks are back in fashion now, didn't you know that?' she said, laughing as she handed him her jacket. 'But I promise to remember that you don't like them. How about a nice Bakelite radiogram as a talking point?'

'I'll give the job to someone else,' he threatened, and disappeared to make the coffee.

Rosalind wandered into the sitting room and spread her plans out on the table. She'd also brought some samples of fabrics and colours, and she displayed these on various chairs so that when Troy came in the rather soulless little room had taken on quite a different atmosphere.

'Good lord.' He stopped on the threshold. 'You've made a difference already! You know, I could almost live with this just as it is.'

'It's only samples,' she laughed. 'Give me *carte blanche* and I could make even this house into something special. Now come and tell me what you think of this.'

He looked over her plans carefully and nodded. She explained her idea for interesting one of the glossies and his enthusiasm was apparent. 'You'd need "before" photos as well as "afters",' he said. 'As it happens, I've got some—I took them for my own interest. I suppose they'd do?'

'I should think so. They're always used as small insets anyway—it's the main pictures of the finished article that the magazines feature most. So you don't mind my approaching an editor or two?'

'Not at all.' He touched her arm. 'Now, come and sit down and drink your coffee and tell me what you've been doing since I saw you last—what was it, three or four years ago?'

'Two weeks,' she said with a smile. 'As you know perfectly well.' Did he realise that his light touch had sent a tingle through her arm and set her skin prickling? She sat down, hesitating for a moment between the rather small sofa and a chair, and chose the chair. Troy flung himself down on the sofa, crossing his long legs and giving her a rather quizzical glance, and she had an uncomfortable feeling that he knew just what was in her mind.

'Well?' he said, and she realised with a start that he was waiting for an answer. 'Just what have you been up to?'

'Oh—nothing much. James was home last weekend, of course.' Why 'of course'? It seemed as if it were becoming an event rather than the norm. 'Other than that, I've just been working. On your scheme,' she added with a quick grin.

'Amongst others, I've no doubt.' He looked at her, frowning slightly. 'Are you telling me you've done nothing but work? What do you do in the evenings, all on your own there?'

'Oh, nothing much. By the time I get back to the flat, all I really want to do is have a bath and a meal and go to bed. Perhaps watch a little TV—think of what I'm going to be doing at work next day. Do a few chores—you know the sort of thing.'

'Heaven forfend that I should know anything of the kind!' he said forcibly. 'Rosalind, it all sounds far too dull for a girl like you. No parties? No dinners out with admiring escorts? No theatres?'

She shook her head, laughing a little. 'No. No parties—or not many, anyway. We all work far too hard, and a lot of the people I know don't actually live in London anyway. They come in each day—haven't you ever heard of commuters? As for the theatre, I love it but I don't much like going alone.'

'And the dinners with admiring escorts? Who might also take you to the theatre?'

'I'm married,' she reminded him. 'I don't *have* admiring escorts.'

He gazed at her and she felt uncomfortable and looked down at her shoes. Her last two sentences rang in her ears. There was a paradox there, one she didn't want to face.

'You ought to have,' he said at last. 'One, at least ... But failing the presence of your husband, who is no doubt taking exactly the same line with regard to his evenings and *never* goes to—let's say the *Folies Bergeres* or the Café de Paris alone ... well, would you allow *me*, perhaps, to act as an escort some evening? Dinner somewhere quiet—a show, maybe? What do you say?'

Rosalind looked at him. She hardly knew how to answer. The idea of going out to dinner with Troy Ballard, of sitting with him close beside her in a darkened theatre, was oddly disturbing. Exciting—and slightly dangerous.

Yet why shouldn't she accept? She was here in his house, she was working with him, and he had made no unwelcome advances. Even after her impulsive kiss, the last time they'd been together, had been accepted as no more that that. He had held her lightly, smiled down at her, and then put her gently away from him. There had been no suggestion that he might have followed it up, or taken advantage in any way.

'Perhaps the idea is so repugnant to you that you can't find words to refuse it,' he said gently, and she laughed in spite of herself.

'It's not repugnant at all—and you know it. As a matter of fact, I'd love to do it sometime when you're in London. It sounds fun. But do you go up very often?'

'Oh, now and then. As it happens, I shall be there the week after next. Some business I have to attend to—a couple of meetings, that kind of thing.' He leaned over the back of the sofa to where his jacket lay across a chair, and his long fingers reached for and found a diary in the pocket. 'Yes, I'll be free on the Tuesday evening—how about you?'

'Yes—that would be fine.' She felt slightly giddy, as if she were being swept along on a strong tidal current. In her single days, she reflected ruefully, she would never readily have admitted to having an evening free. There would have been much searching in her own diary, much pondering. But she was married now—and Troy already knew, or suspected, the loneliness of her spare time.

'That's wonderful. So if you'll give me

directions, I'll come and pick you up—let's say about seven, shall we? Does that give you time to get home and have a rest before getting ready? I don't want you rushing.'

'No, that's fine.' She could finish work early that evening, get home at six, shower and change ... 'Yes, I can be ready at seven.'

'Theatre first and then supper somewhere,' he decreed. 'Tell me if there's anything you *don't* want to see. And now', he drained his coffee mug and set it back on the tray, '—let's have a really good look at these plans of yours. And then we'll go and see what—if anything— has been done to the cottage since last time you saw it. And after that—well, if you're in no hurry to get back to your mama, I thought we might have a drive around some of the villages. Go for a walk, perhaps. Find a spot of tea. And—'

'And then you're invited back to dinner with us,' Rosalind said, making up her mind. It had been the last thing Sheila had said to her as she left that morning—'Don't forget to ask Troy back for supper.'——but she'd been uncertain, not quite sure of how they stood.

Now, she had forgotten her doubts. They were friends, she enjoyed his company and she was going to meet him in London in ten days' time. So why shouldn't he come back to the cottage this evening?

Somehow, it seemed to set the seal of respectability on it. James could hardly, after

110

all, object to a friendship which had so positively been given her own mother's approval.

Not that he'd be likely to know anyway, she thought with a stab of bitterness. He was always too interested in his own projects these days to enquire about hers. And somehow they both kept off the subject of what went on in their spare time.

CHAPTER SIX

Of course, the traffic would have to be worse that evening than on any other. Hot and irritated, Rosalind drove at last into the car-park under the flats and switched off the engine. She had less than an hour to get ready for her date with Troy. And she'd so much wanted to appear cool and unhurried when he arrived!

Well, she still could. She'd spent the previous evening deciding which outfit to wear and the cool, dark blue linen dress was hanging up ready for her to slide into. All she had to do was shower, slick on a little lipstick and eyeshadow, and she would look as if she'd done nothing but lie on her little balcony in the sun all day. And since Troy knew perfectly well that in fact she held down a busy job, that was just the impression she wanted to give.

It was disconcerting, therefore, to come out of the shower just in time to hear the telephone ringing in the sitting room.

Rosalind hesitated. Why not just let it ring? But it might be Troy, ringing to say he'd be late for some reason. She wrapped a big, pale blue towel around her wet body and crossed the room to pick it up.

'Oh, hullo, darling.' It was James. 'Look, I just thought I'd ring you before you settle down to work.'

A trifle guiltily, she remembered that she'd let him think that was how she planned to spend her evenings this week. Somehow the subject of her date with Troy had never come up.

'I forgot to bring some papers with me. Plans of the *chateau* conversion. I need them by Thursday—d'you think you could root them out?'

'Yes, I suppose so. But how am I going to get them to you by Thursday? It's Tuesday now.'

'I know. Stupid of me, but I wanted to show them to you or I'd never have brought them.' There was a note of reproach in his voice. He'd tried two or three times to show her the plans, but she'd brushed aside his efforts, still angry with him, wanting to make him realise she just wasn't interested. So now she was going to be blamed because he'd forgotten to take them back, was she?

Her voice was cold when she spoke again.

'Yes, it was rather silly, wasn't it. So how do you suggest I send them? Or do you want me to drop everything and fly over to Paris myself?'

'Good lord no, don't do that!' His reaction was so quick, it was insulting. Rosalind felt a flare of anger. 'No, it's all right, Lisa can bring them, she—'

'*Lisa?*'

'Yes—she took an extra couple of days on the weekend. I didn't need her too badly—' He could have phrased that better, Rosalind thought sourly. 'And her mother's been a bit off-colour, so I suggested she stay on. Anyway, she's flying over tomorrow so she can drop in and collect the papers this evening, if that's all right.'

Rosalind opened her mouth to speak and then closed it again. No, it most certainly was *not* all right! But she could hardly tell James that now. She cast wildly about in her mind. Couldn't she just say she was going out with a friend? But he was sure to ask which friend, and she couldn't bring herself to lie to him.

Nor could she tell him she was going out with Troy Ballard.

'Rosalind?' he said. 'Are you still there?'

'Yes—yes, I'm still here.'

'Well, will you do that, then?' he asked, a trifle impatiently. 'Find the papers and give them to Lisa when she arrives?'

'Yes—yes, I suppose so.' She gathered herself together. 'Actually, I was thinking of

113

going out—it's such a lovely evening here. I—I thought I might go out for a meal—walk or something.' It was almost the truth, but she knew it wasn't really. And her voice had sounded so weak and lame, James would surely suspect something. 'You don't know what time she might come, I suppose?' she asked desperately.

'No, I don't,' James said. Was she imagining it, or had his voice chilled? Was he annoyed that she was planning to go out? The anger flared again. Why *shouldn't* she go out if she felt like it? Come to that, why shouldn't she go out with Troy? This wasn't the Victorian age, after all. Men and women could go out together for an evening without the wrong construction being put on it—couldn't they?

'I suppose you could ring her mother's home and see if she's there,' James added. 'But since she's not well, it might be a nuisance to her. Do you have to go out this evening, Ros? Couldn't you make it tomorrow?'

'It might be raining tomorrow,' she said feebly, and glanced at her watch. Troy would be here in fifteen minutes! So much for her being ready when he arrived, cool and unflustered. 'James, this call must be costing a bomb—'

'Well, I've got to know what you intend to do about these papers,' he stated. 'Are you going to wait in for Lisa or not? She may be on her way there now, for all I know—it won't completely ruin your evening. I can't see why you're so desperate to go out tonight anyway. You're not meeting anyone else, are you?'

Rosalind knew that he didn't mean 'are you meeting another man?' He meant was she meeting a girl friend. But she dared not say yes. It would only lead to more complications.

She took refuge in the anger that was warring with guilt inside her. 'What if I were? Doesn't it occur to you, James, that I don't have to sit indoors night after night just because you're not here? I do have a life of my own to lead, you know. And if I feel like going out tonight, I don't see why I shouldn't be free to do just that—whether I'm meeting anyone else or not. I don't see why I have to stay in to wait for your secretary to turn up just when she feels like it, to collect some papers you've been stupid enough to leave behind and should never have brought in the first place!'

There was a short silence. Then James said icily, 'Very well, Rosalind, if that's the way you feel. The papers aren't essential anyway—it's just a slight embarrassment that I haven't got them. But I quite see that I have no right to expect you to set aside your own desires just to help me.' And he put down the phone.

Rosalind stood with the receiver pressed to her ear, stunned and dismayed. She and James had never quarrelled in this way before. She felt as if her heart had been torn from her breast, shredded with rough, uncaring fingers and then jammed back again. She even put her hand up, feeling the place where it beat so raggedly, as if expecting to find some ends hanging untidily out.

Oh James, James, she thought, what's happening to us?

She put the phone back slowly, then picked it up again. Her finger was already on the button, beginning to dial the code for Paris, when the doorbell rang. She dropped the receiver and lifted both hands to her cheeks.

Troy! He was here, a few minutes early. She looked down at the blue towel that was wrapped around her. It wasn't exactly how she'd meant to greet him, but it was respectable enough. At least, it covered her as much as the dress she intended to wear. Nevertheless, she was acutely conscious of the fact that she wore nothing underneath it as she went to the door and opened it.

But it wasn't Troy who stood there. It was Lisa.

'Oh!' Rosalind stood staring at her, blankly, before standing back to let her in.

Lisa walked past into the sitting room. She had been here before, of course, for the parties that James and Rosalind occasionally held, and since she had worked for the same firm for as long as they had, Rosalind knew her well. In fact, she'd always rather liked the glamorous secretary—until the day she'd moved with James to IntInt, and then accompanied him to

Paris.

Now they stood in the white sitting room and eyed each other warily.

'Sorry to barge in,' Lisa said. Her voice was calm and friendly. She'd acquired a new elegance since she'd been in Paris, Rosalind thought, noticing the simple but clearly expensive suit, the shoes that could almost walk by themselves. And her short, dark hair had been differently styled. It fitted her head like a cap, gleaming like polished ebony. 'James said he'd phone you. I have to collect some papers.'

'Oh—yes, he did ring. I've only just put down the phone.' Rosalind felt a sudden surge of relief. If she could only get rid of Lisa before Troy arrived, the evening needn't be spoilt after all, and James would have his precious papers. 'I haven't had time to find them yet,' she went on. 'Can you wait a minute or two while I look in his desk?'

'Yes, of course.' Lisa looked at the towel and smiled. 'I seem to have come at a bad moment. Isn't it always the way, as soon as you get into the bath the phone rings or someone comes to the door. Or both, and you don't know which to answer first.'

'Yes. Sit down for a minute.' Rosalind went through to the study. She ought to have offered Lisa a drink, but that would have only encouraged the other girl to stay, and Rosalind was anxious to get rid of her as quickly as

117

possible. She rummaged hastily through the desk and to her relief found it almost at once. A file, marked with the name of the *chateau*. She picked it up and hurried back to the sitting room.

'Here it is.' She gave a little laugh. 'Men! They'd forget their heads if they weren't screwed on. Good thing they have women to run around after them.'

Lisa was standing at the window, looking out over the park. She turned and held out her hand for the file. 'They would, wouldn't they? Not that I consider my job as "running around" after any man—not even your James. I mean to make a career just as much as any other woman these days. Being a secretary is just one rung on the ladder.'

She gave Rosalind a charming smile. 'We have to look after ourselves, we single girls. Anyway,' she moved towards the door, 'I can see you don't want visitors, so I'll be going. Thanks for finding the papers.'

'That's all right.' They were half-way across the room when the doorbell rang again. Rosalind jumped slightly and couldn't prevent an almost guilty glance towards Lisa. Now this almost certainly *was* Troy—and just what was she going to think?

More important, what was she going to tell James?

I wish I'd told him myself now, Rosalind thought agonisedly. But there was nothing to be done about it. Nor was there any way out of answering the door. Lisa was already looking at her a little strangely, no doubt wondering why she wasn't hurrying to see who her caller was. She took a fresh grip on her towel, made sure it was tucked in securely over her breasts, and went through to the little hall.

Troy was just about the press the bell again. He took his finger away from the button, raised his eyebrows slightly and handed her a bunch of white roses. 'Well, I like the outfit! But is it really what the smart theatregoer is wearing these days?'

He stepped past her and glanced appreciatively around the hall. 'Very nice. I can see you're going to make a real success of the cottage—can't wait to move in.'

Rosalind showed him through to the sitting room. The whole thing had now become a nightmare and there was nothing she could do but hope to wake up soon.

She looked at Lisa, who was still standing politely in the middle of the room, and wished it were she who was wearing the smart Parisian suit and Italian shoes. Bath towels simply couldn't compete ... 'This is Troy Ballard,' she said foolishly. 'A—a friend of my mother's.' Lisa's eyes widened at that, and she saw Troy's mouth twitch. 'And this is Lisa Marsh, my husband's secretary. She just came in to collect some papers.'

'And now I must be going.' Lisa smiled into

Troy's eyes. She had given him her hand and he was still holding it. Or was she still holding his? By now, Rosalind hardly cared. She was uneasily afraid that the towel was beginning to slip. And why shouldn't it? If this were a TV comedy, as well as a nightmare, it would be exactly what would happen next. She put her fingers on the top, hoping that the gesture looked casual, and gave it a little tug.

'I seem to have held things up,' Lisa was saying now. 'I'm sure Rosalind would have been ready by now if I hadn't had to come for these silly papers. Did you say you were going to the theatre?'

'Yes, to see the latest Lloyd Webber.' Troy glanced at his watch, then at Rosalind. 'We don't actually have much time—I'm afraid I was a bit late myself—so if you—'

'Oh—yes, of course. And I'll put these lovely roses in some water.' Rosalind escaped into the bedroom and shut the door, remembering then that she hadn't shown Lisa out. Well, perhaps the girl would have the sense to find her own way to the door. But she had a feeling that there had been more than friendly interest in Lisa's eyes when she held out her hand to Troy, and she wasn't a bit surprised to come out of the bedroom twenty minutes later to find the two of them sitting on the sofa and chatting as if they'd known each other all their lives.

'Good lord, you're ready and I'm still here!' Lisa jumped to her feet, all pretty apology. 'I'm so sorry, Rosalind. I ought to have gone by now anyway—I've got a thousand things to do at home.' She made to go out but Troy put out a hand to detain her.

'Don't rush off. We can give you a lift part of the way. My car's down in the street.' He smiled at Rosalind. 'That's all right, isn't it? Lisa's been telling me where she lives—it'll only take us five minutes to drop her off.'

'Quite all right,' Rosalind muttered. She saw them out on to the landing and locked the door behind her. The three of them went down in the lift together and walked to Troy's car. Lisa slid into the back seat, showing rather more leg than Rosalind thought necessary, and began to give directions.

'Well, that's our duty done,' Troy said at last when she had slid out again and they'd watched her sway down the street in her tight Parisian suit and high heels. 'Now we can enjoy ourselves! I haven't told you yet just how lovely you look in that dress, Rosalind. Come to that—' and a wicked smile curved his chiselled lips, '—I never told you how lovely you looked in that rather precarious bath towel . . .' and his eyes smiled lazily, seductively, into hers.

Rosalind gazed back at him. Her heart had begun to thump again, her skin to tingle, and her lips felt dry. So Lisa's charms hadn't had any effect on him after all. And now the evening lay before them like a glittering jewel, not spoiled in the least.

She smiled and relaxed. And prepared to enjoy herself.

*   *   *

'That was a wonderful evening, Troy.' She stopped at her door, leaning back and looking up into his face. 'I don't know when I've enjoyed myself so much. The show was marvellous, and the supper out of this world. How did you know about that place?'

He grinned and tapped his nose. 'It's a well-kept secret between me and a few friends. We don't want everyone knowing about it—just enough of us to make it worth while the proprietor's keeping it open! So don't go spreading it around, will you—next thing you know, it'll be in one of those Good Eating Guides, filled to choking point with provincials and the prices going up with the latest rocket.'

Rosalind laughed. 'You know, there are times when I suspect you're something of a snob.' She hesitated a little, then said lightly, 'Coffee?'

'I thought you'd never ask,' Troy remarked, and slid through the door after her.

Rosalind felt her heart thump a little raggedly as she slipped out of her evening jacket and dropped it across a chair. She wasn't at all sure this was a good idea, and she knew very well that James would definitely not approve. Coming in 'for coffee' was a euphemism for something else these days, wasn't it? But surely Troy would understand that she meant just that—coffee. After all, in spite of his sometimes wicked grin and sideways glances, he hadn't made any real advances towards her. And he knew she was married. Happily married, she added silently and went swiftly towards the kitchen.

'That new girl in the leading role is very good, isn't she?' she called over her shoulder, and then found that Troy had followed her and was standing at the door. 'Oh, sorry, I thought you were still in the sitting room. What do you think, was she better than the original?'

'Well, the original is always a hard act to follow.' He was leaning against the door jamb, watching her as she moved about setting the coffee-maker, placing bone china mugs on a tray. 'But yes, I thought she was very good. Especially in the dancing scene.'

He moved closer and began to hum the tune of the waltz to which the leading characters had danced. Then he slid his arms around Rosalind's waist and drew her close against him, into the dance. His head bent to hers and she felt his cheek against her hair.

Rosalind stiffened momentarily. Then she relaxed. What was worrying her anyway? It was just a dance—just a little fun, that was all. And it was pleasant here in Troy's arms. She could feel the strong, lean length of him, the movement of his muscles as he drew her closer

123

and rocked her gently in time to his humming. She could feel his breath against her ear, the soft movements of his lips as he whispered the words of the love song. She turned her head slightly; felt his mouth move across her cheek, touch her own soft, trembling lips...

The shrill sound of the telephone sliced through the air. Troy stopped humming abruptly. But he did not let Rosalind go. Instead, his arms seemed, almost imperceptibly, to tighten around her slender body.

Rosalind put her hands on his arms and tried to push him away. 'Please, Troy—let me go.'

'Don't answer it,' he muttered, his lips still close to her face. 'Just ignore it, Rosalind. Let it ring.'

'But I must answer it! It must be James. Troy, it's gone midnight, he'll be frantic if he doesn't get an answer.' She pushed again at his arms and this time he let her go.

Breathless, she ran into the sitting room and picked up the phone. 'Hullo? James? Is that you?'

'No, it's not James, it's me.' *Lisa's* voice. 'Rosalind, I'm so sorry to ring you so late, only I've been trying ever since ten. I thought you might be back early.' She sounded almost panic-stricken. 'Rosalind, would you believe I got home and found I didn't have that file after all! Did I leave it in your flat, or was it in the car? I just can't remember. And James will go

124

mad if I've lost it.' She really was frantic.

Rosalind had a brief, almost pleasurable vision of the cool, sophisticated Lisa in the kind of demented flap of a young and not very efficient typist who has lost an important document.

Then her better feelings took over and she spoke soothingly into the receiver. At least it hadn't been James, wanting an explanation as to where she'd been until after twelve-thirty in the morning ... 'Calm down, Lisa, I'll have a look. I'm sure it wasn't in the car.' She put the phone down and glanced around the room.

Troy, who had followed her in and heard her words, went over to the side table. He picked up the file and held it out, his eyebrows raised interrogatively.

Rosalind nodded. 'It's all right,' she said into the receiver. 'It's here. Now what d'you want me to do with it? Will you be able to call in for it in the morning?'

'No, I won't.' Lisa sounded relieved but still almost as despairing as before. 'I've got to catch the earliest plane and I can't leave Mother until my sister arrives to look after her, and she won't be here until the last moment ... Well, James will just have to manage without them. I'll explain it to him somehow. Or—just a minute!' There was a tiny lift of hope in her voice.

Rosalind waited a moment. Troy had come close to her and slid his arm around her waist.

She moved away slightly, feeling uncomfortable, and said politely into the phone: 'Well? Have you thought of something?'

'Yes. I don't know. It's just—well, there's someone who might be coming over to Paris tomorrow by a later plane. He could perhaps collect the file from you and bring it. Yes, that's it. I'll ring him first thing and ask him. He could probably call in at Lords & Ladies. Would that be all right, Rosalind? Would you mind taking it to work with you?'

'No, I don't mind. Look, tell you what, you give me your friend's phone number and I'll ring him for you. That'll save you the trouble when you've already got so much to do.' It really did sound as if poor Lisa had a lot on her plate, and if her mother were really ill...

She found a pencil and paper and took down the number that Lisa dictated to her. Then she cut off the other girl's effusive thanks with a quick, 'That's OK, Lisa. See you soon,' and hung up.

'This wretched file!' she said, taking it out of Troy's hands and dropping it on the sofa. 'It's more trouble than it's worth. Why James ever had to bring it home, I just don't know. Him and his *chateau*!' She turned and gave Troy a smile. 'I'd rather be designing a nice interior for a Cotswold cottage any day. But now—no.'

She pushed him gently away. 'I really must ask you to go now, Troy. Just a quick cup of coffee—it must be made by now—and then good-night. I do have an awful lot to do tomorrow.'

He made a face of resignation. 'Oh, all right. I know when I'm beaten. But we'll do this again sometime, yes? The theatre and dinner? I've really enjoyed it, Rosalind.'

'So have I. It's been lovely.' She went back to the kitchen, poured the coffee and brought it into the sitting room.

They drank it quickly, keeping their conversation light, and then Troy stood up to leave. 'I'll be in touch, Rosalind.'

She saw him to the door and he paused, tipped her chin up with one finger and gave her a quick, light kiss. 'No one I'd rather spend an evening with,' he said, and his next kiss was more lingering, tender, searching. He lifted his face away and looked into her eyes and she knew that hers were as dark and as serious as his. 'Soon,' he murmured, and then he was gone.

Rosalind closed the door quietly and leaned against it. She lifted her hand to touch her lips, expecting to find them burning. But the kisses had been light enough, cool enough. And the touch of his hands on her body had been equally light. There was really no need for this tingling, this sensation of having been touched by fire. No need at all.

It had been a good-night kiss, nothing more, after a pleasant evening enjoying each other's company. There was no more to it than that.

So why, suddenly, did she have this almost unbearable need for James? Why was she suddenly shaken by a desire to pick up the phone and hear his voice? To have him here with her, his arms about her, his lips on hers with the familiarity that was yet still so exciting? Why did she suddenly want him so badly?

Trembling with unexpected longing, she walked into the sitting room and picked up the file that still lay where she had dropped it. She stared at it for a long while, and then she knew what she must do.

*   *   *

The scheduled flight to Paris left exactly on time and Rosalind settled back in her seat. In a couple of hours she would be in James's office. Just in time for lunch. She smiled at the thought of his astonishment when he saw her. And—she hoped—his pleasure.

It had been a busy morning, making all the arrangements: calling the airport to reserve the flight, letting the office know she was taking two days' leave—for she couldn't go to Paris and not stay the night!—calling the number Lisa had given her to tell the friend, whoever he was, that he wouldn't need to collect the file after all. The only person she hadn't called was James. But, in the last few minutes before she left, she'd picked up the phone on impulse and dialled the number of an exchange in the Cotswolds.

'You're going to Paris?' her mother exclaimed. 'This morning? That's rather sudden, isn't it?'

'Not really. And it's no big deal, after all. Paris is only a hop, skip and jump away. Why shouldn't I pop over now and then to see my husband?'

'Well, of course there's no reason.' But Sheila still sounded doubtful. 'And you young people think nothing of doing things we older ones would have thought about for months. But you will take care, won't you, darling? I mean, you've never actually travelled alone and—'

'I shall be perfectly all right, Mother.' Rosalind felt the familiar exasperation crawl over her skin. 'Nothing can go wrong. Airlines don't let you get lost or board the wrong plane or anything like that—it's easier than travelling by train. You can even understand the announcements. Anyway, I've got to go now. I just thought I ought to let you know.'

'Yes, of course. Well, have a lovely time, darling, and look after yourself. Give James my love.' Rosalind heard the 'ping' of the shop door. 'Oh, I'll have to go now—customer.' And Sheila put down her phone.

Well, that was that. Rosalind too had replaced her receiver, feeling faintly irritated as she so often did after talking with her mother, and gone down to the car park.

And now here she was, high above the Channel, the precious file safely in the overnight bag that was all the luggage she had brought, feeling almost as excited as a child on its first visit to the seaside.

Anyone would think, she reflected with amusement, that it was three years since she had seen her husband instead of only three days. And for the first time since last night, she allowed herself to think briefly of Troy Ballard.

It had been a very pleasant evening. An evening she could easily be persuaded to repeat. But it wouldn't do. She knew that now.

There was a quality about Troy, a promise of excitement, an allurement, that spelt danger. Last night she'd been tempted by that promise of excitement, that air of danger.

Now, she could only thank Lisa for that frantic, late-night phone call. It had saved her from possibly making a mistake she would have regretted for the rest of her life.

That was why she'd needed James so badly—to reinforce her belief in herself, in their love. That was why she was on her way to Paris now, instead of giving the file to Lisa's friend. That was why she was gazing down at the grey, hammered surface of the Channel, urging the plane on in her mind, praying that there would be no delays.

That was why she planned to stay overnight.

*   *   *

There were no delays. The flight was smooth and uneventful, and by eleven-thirty Rosalind was in a taxi, fighting the Paris traffic. She found herself at the door to James's office just before twelve.

The office was in a large block in the business area, and she had to read a long column of names before she came to IntInt. Then she gave her name to the bored receptionist in the large, marble hallway and took the lift to the appropriate floor.

The door to the IntInt offices was opposite the lift. Her heart now almost in her mouth, Rosalind knocked and went in. She looked around for her husband.

The office was large and open-plan. There were small divisions made by tall potted plants, shelves and filing cabinets. She had to walk around, uneasily conscious of raised heads and watching eyes, wondering just where James's desk was. Or did he have an office to himself? Maybe she was in the wrong place after all. Maybe he wasn't even here today. And where was Lisa?

A girl got up from one of the desks and came over to her. She was small and impossibly thin, with hair cut like a street urchin's, yet she still managed to exude an indefinable aura of style and elegance that made Rosalind, in her best linen skirt and jacket, feel frumpily overdressed. In French, she asked if Rosalind wanted any help and Rosalind searched amongst her memories for the right phrase.

'*Je cherche mon mari.*' Was that right? '*Je suis Mme* Camarthey.'

'Ah, *M* Camarthey.' The girl nodded and beckoned. '*Ici, Madame.*' She led the way to a door in the corner of the big office and knocked, giving Rosalind a wide grin as she did so and looking even more like a *gamine*. Then she opened the door. '*Mme* Camarthey, *monsieur.*'

'*Mme who?*'

Rosalind heard James's tone of astonishment, but before the giggling girl could say any more she had pushed past and was in the room. She rushed forward to fling herself into his arms. Half-laughing, half-crying, she clung to him, kissing his face, talking incoherently about the file, Lisa, the aeroplane. 'Oh, James, James...' Again she thought that it was as if they had been parted for years.

James disentangled her arms from around his neck. He gave her a kiss—a brief, cool kiss. With a sudden feeling of dismay, she looked at him and realised, horrifyingly, that he wasn't pleased to see her at all. He was disconcerted. He was annoyed. He was *embarrassed*.

Embarrassed? To see his *wife*?

Rosalind stepped back. She felt suddenly

cold, cold right through to her bones, as if she had been out for days in a storm of ice and snow and would never be warm again. She looked at the chill in James's eyes and then, slowly, she looked around the room.

Lisa was there, looking as if she wished the floor would open up and swallow her. And there were two other people, people Rosalind didn't know and was sure James had never mentioned to her.

A big, swarthy man, obviously French and obviously rich. Gold glittered on his fingers and on his wrist and, when he opened his mouth, in his teeth. He was watching her narrowly, and there was displeasure in his face.

And the other was a girl, a few years younger than herself—twenty-one or twenty-two, Rosalind guessed. A girl as exquisite as a fairy doll, slender and tiny, with a cascade of silvery fair hair and a figure that looked as if it were made of fine spun glass.

She was looking at James. And she looked as if she owned him.

CHAPTER SEVEN

In the silence that followed her eruption into the office, Rosalind could hear the thunder of the Paris traffic far below. She saw that behind James was a large window, through which

133

could be seen the cathedral of Notre-Dame, its towers proud and regal above the loops of the Seine. She looked at the faces around the room and thought that they looked even stonier than those ancient towers.

'Forgive me,' the swarthy man said politely. 'I did not know that you were expecting your wife to join us, *m'sieur* Camarthey.'

'Neither did I,' James said, and held out his hand, taking Rosalind by the elbow and turning her to face the others. 'Rosalind, this is my client *M* Ferrer. His daughter, *Mlle* Ginette. *Monsieur, mademoiselle, c'est ma femme*, Rosalind.'

'Let us speak in English if it is easier for you,' *M* Ferrer said, taking her hand. His accent was guttural but his grammar good, and Rosalind could understand him. She smiled gratefully, though still feeling close to tears with humiliation, and turned to his daughter.

Ginette's hand was so small and slender that Rosalind was almost afraid of breaking the delicate bones. She looked up at Rosalind with eyes like freshly opened cornflowers in a face as smoothly perfect as porcelain, just faintly touched with dew. Her lips were a pale, soft rose, and they parted to reveal teeth as tiny as a child's.

She looks as if she'd just stepped down from a Christmas tree, Rosalind thought, and found her eyes going to James's face.

And immediately wished she hadn't.

134

Because the expression on his face was one she hadn't seen for months. It was an expression of love so tender that it made her heart ache to see it. It was an expression of desire and passion and hunger. It was an expression she had seen when he looked at her in the park in sunlight, or in a country lane by the light of the moon. Or in their bedroom, when he held her in his arms and made love to her.

And it was directed now, not at her, but at the fairy creature who stood with Rosalind's hand touching hers, who smiled up at her with a rosebud mouth and opened wide, cornflower eyes fringed with long, dusky black lashes.

I was wrong to worry about Lisa, Rosalind thought dully, and she looked across the room to see Lisa watching her with what looked very like pity in her eyes.

And then she lifted her chin and turned back to face her husband, to face the look that told her all. 'I brought your file, James,' she said quietly, and laid it on his desk. 'I'm sorry—I just came on impulse, I didn't meant to interrupt. I—I'll go now.' And she turned, blindly, to leave the office.

There was immediate consternation. Lisa gave an exclamation, *M* Ferrer started forward and James came quickly forward and caught her shoulders. He turned her towards him and kissed her firmly on the lips. 'Don't be ridiculous, Ros. You didn't come all this way just to turn round and go home again. Look, we were just going out to lunch. You'll come with us and then I can finish my business with *M* Ferrer and take you back to the apartment. When do you go back? I presume you've already arranged it.'

You *hope* I've already arranged it, Rosalind thought miserably, but she smiled brightly and said, too quickly, 'I've booked a flight tomorrow evening, but of course I can always bring it forward. I'm sure there'll be room on an afternoon flight today. I know you're probably busy, you often work late in the evenings, don't you? I don't want to be a nuisance.'

'I told you, don't be silly.' He spoke brusquely and her heart ached for the tenderness she had seen in his face. Had she really lost him? Was there nothing she could do to win him back? He turned to *M* Ferrer and spoke rapidly to him in French.

They carried on an animated conversation for a few minutes, a conversation which left Rosalind floundering, and then James turned back to her. 'We're all going to the ballet tonight,' he said. '*M* Ferrer has booked a box and he says there'll be plenty of room for you too, so there's no problem about seats. Have you brought anything to wear?'

'Not to the ballet. I didn't think—'

'Of course not.'

As if it were too much to expect that she could think at all!

'Well, there may be time for some shopping after lunch. But now we'd better go. Lisa, is there a car organised?'

The secretary spoke for the first time. 'Yes, it's all ready and waiting.' She gave Rosalind an apologetic glance and whispered as they went out of the office, 'I'm terribly sorry, Rosalind. I'd no idea you meant to come yourself. I could have warned James—'

'I wanted it to be a surprise.' But the surprise had backfired, she thought miserably, and wished she had simply let Lisa's friend bring the file. Then she would never have known about the dainty, fairy-child that James had so clearly fallen in love with. Never have seen that look of blazing, tender passion directed at another woman.

But that was stupid! She would have known sometime. Because it was quite clear that her marriage was over. That look didn't happen on the face of a man who was simply having an affair. That expression, seen on James's face, was for real.

And tiny, fairylike and delicate Ginette Ferrer might be, but there was a look on her face that was equally unmistakable.

It was the look of a predator.

*　　*　　*

'Well, you certainly chose the right day to come flying over on a surprise visit.' James led

137

Rosalind into the apartment and switched on the lights. 'Ballet at the *Opera* was something quite special.' He went to the window to draw the curtains across the sparkling carpet of lights that stretched away to the horizon, and then came back to take Rosalind's arms in his hands. 'And now perhaps you can tell me what this is all about.'

'What *what's* all about?' She stared up at him, hoping to convey a look of bland innocence. 'I don't know what you're talking about, James.'

'You do. You know very well what I'm talking about. There was no need for you to come rushing across the Channel just to bring me that file. Lisa had already explained that a friend of hers could bring it. In fact, it wasn't that desperately urgent after all, though we didn't know that last night. But you certainly didn't have to ditch your own work to bring it. What did they think at Lords & Ladies?'

'They didn't think anything at all. They know I'm up to date enough with my work to take a day or two off if I feel like it. And why shouldn't I come over to see you, James? I don't seem to have interrupted your work, after all. Lunch going on until three in the afternoon, time for a little shopping with me, the ballet and dinner in the evening—not exactly a punishing schedule, is it?'

'Today happened to be an exception—' he began, but she broke in.

'I should hope it was! After all your protestations about how hard you work, I wouldn't like to think this goes on all the time. And does the little Ginette feature largely in your workload?'

James sighed and turned up his eyes. 'I might have known you'd fasten on to that. Ginette just happens to be *M* Ferrer's daughter and comes with him when he comes to discuss the work we're doing for him. He has a house in Paris and another in the country, so he's an important client—I don't want to offend him. And—'

'And it's normal for a client to entertain you with lunch and the ballet? Sounds a little over the top to me, James. And from the way that girl looked at you—'

'Ginette's no more than a child,' he said crisply. 'Rosalind, if you think I'm even contemplating an affair with her, you're even more foolish than I thought. I—'

'So you do think I'm foolish!' Tears of bitter pain stung her eyes. 'James, do you hear what you're saying? Oh, I wish I'd never come.' She turned away from him, brushing the tears away with the palm of her hand but unable to stop their flow. 'I thought you'd be pleased to see me,' she said with a sob. 'I thought it would be lovely to be here in Paris with you. I thought it would be *romantic.*'

There was a short silence. Then James came close behind her and she felt his hands on her shoulders. He drew her back against his body and his lips touched her ear. 'Ros—darling— don't sound so unhappy. Of course I'm glad you came—I was just surprised, that's all. And worried, in case you thought—well, that anything might be going on. It isn't, Ros, I swear to you it isn't. I love you.'

He turned her, gently, to face him. 'You believe that, don't you? I love you? I love you. There's nobody else for me—nobody. Never has been, never will be.' He bent and touched her lips with his, brushing them very gently, tenderly, letting his tongue flick across them as softly as moonlight. 'Believe me?' he whispered, and one hand moved on her body to touch her breast.

'Oh, *James*,' she gasped, and her arms went round his neck. She clung to him, pressing her body close, feeling the arousal in him and moving against him in response. His lips were on hers again and she let her mouth part, giving herself up to his kiss. She felt his tongue run swiftly, delicately, around the soft inner skin of her lips, and let her own come forward to meet it. His hand was on her breast, teasing the nipple into thrusting excitement, and she twisted in his arms and whimpered softly.

'Ros...' James's voice was little more than a growl, the purring growl of a great cat. He lifted her in his arms and carried her through to the bedroom. The only light in here was from the moon, shining in through the uncurtained window. It lay in a broad silver shaft across the bed, and James laid Rosalind down in its gleaming light and bent to unfasten the dress he had bought her only that afternoon.

She lay naked in the glimmering room and watched as he stripped off his own clothes. It was only three nights since they had last been together, yet she felt as tremulous, as nervously excited, as a young bride.

James turned and came towards her. The moonlight rippled across his muscles as he moved, lit a sheen on his black hair. His dark eyes were shadowed but as he bent towards her she caught the shine in them and knew that they moved over her body, taking in every silver-lit line of it, and she could almost feel their caress over her breasts, down the slight swell of her stomach and on the soft, delicate skin of her thighs.

She shivered, almost unable to bear the tension any longer, and felt a relief that was mixed with soaring excitement as he lay beside her and took her closely in his arms. 'James,' she whispered as she wound her arms about him and twined her legs with his. 'James, I've missed you ... so much...'

'I know.' He slid his fingers gently down her spine, barely touching her skin, so that she moved and arched against him. 'I know. I've missed you too. What's been happening to us, Ros?'

She shook her head, burying her face against

his neck. 'Don't talk about it. Don't talk at all. Just love me, James—love me. Please.' And she pressed herself closer still, tightening her limbs about him as if to make contact with every possible fragment of skin. Her need rose in her, urgent, desperate, almost frightening.

Lifting her face, she found his mouth with hers and drove her tongue into his mouth, exploring, searching, demanding. Her body moved against his and she was aware of every muscle, every contour, hardening against her, his lean body responding with a swift virility that matched and transcended hers so that, passionate as she was, it was James who began to lead the way, to arouse and tease and drive them on, now lifting her to the brink of a height that had her gasping, now letting her gently down to a plateau where she lay whimpering, mutely begging, now raising her again to a peak of sensation that was almost intolerable ... Then at last it broke, crashing about their ears, bringing them back down to earth, back to the soft, French bed somewhere in the middle of Paris where they lay stranded, breathless and exhausted, yet still wrapped closely together and reluctant for a long time to part.

At last, Rosalind stirred. She turned slightly in James's arms and smiled into his face. But the moonlight had moved on and no longer shone into the room. She took his hand and traced his finger along the curve of her lips, making the shape of a broad, upturned grin, and he laughed softly.

'The cat that got the cream! Better now, Ros?'

'Better,' she whispered. 'I'm sorry, James.'

'I'm sorry too. Though I'm not quite sure what either of us is sorry for.' He kissed her gently. 'Feel like some sleep?'

'Mm.' She settled herself comfortably against him, and felt herself drifting away. He lay behind her, his body fitted around her like a spoon, and she covered his arms with hers. His skin was warm against hers.

When the telephone buzzed beside the bed, she barely heard it. It was James's movements as he half-turned to lift it from its rest that roused her. Snuggling close, still half dazed, she listened, and heard a voice from the receiver, a voice that she recognised. A voice that she had never heard until today, but which seemed, tiny as it was, to fill the room.

''As she gone, James? Or is she still there?' The charming French accent lilted in Rosalind's unbelieving ears. 'Oh James, I was so disappointed...'

James put down the receiver. He turned immediately to draw Rosalind back into his arms. But she was out of the bed, pulling the covers off to wrap her naked body, searching in the darkness for shoes, for clothes, for anything.

'Ros! Don't! Look, I can explain—'

'Explain *that*?' Her voice was high, angry and bitter as it had never been before. She found the light switch and snapped it on, flooding the room with harsh white light. 'Don't even try, James. I don't want to listen. I've heard enough of your explanations.'

She gave up looking for her clothes and made towards the door. 'I'm going to sleep on the sofa, and *don't* try to stop me. Just leave me alone—*alone*, do you hear?'

She stopped at the door and looked back at him. Tousled, dishevelled, with only a sheet left to cover him, he looked more impossibly, more infuriatingly attractive than ever.

But he didn't attract her—not now. Not ever again. 'If you tried to touch me now,' she said, slowly and clearly, 'I think I would probably be very, very sick.'

And she turned and went through the door, closing it very carefully, very quietly, very firmly, behind her.

*   *   *

The airport was busy even early in the morning, but Rosalind was able to secure a seat on the first flight back to London. She drew in a sigh that was half relief, half a sob, and found herself somewhere to sit while she waited for the flight to be called.

She didn't think she had slept at all. Wrapping herself in the blankets she had

144

dragged from the bed, she had lain on the sofa, staring wide-eyed at the square of light that was the window, watching it become paler as dawn approached.

Her emotions in turmoil, she had found her mind flooded with conflicting ideas. At one moment, she was half off the sofa, ready to go in and shake James awake—she was certain he would have fallen callously asleep—but before her feet touched the floor she was swinging them back on to the sofa again, bitter tears running down her cheeks, knowing that any impulsive action of hers could mean the end of her marriage—the end of all she held most dear.

But wasn't it the end of her marriage anyway? And—to face the painful truth—wasn't it really the case that her marriage had already ended, weeks, perhaps months before? That she and James had been living a charade?

Perhaps it had never been real at all. Perhaps it had always been a terrible mistake...

Tortured by her thoughts, Rosalind could stay on the sofa no longer. She got up, padded over to the window and drew the curtains aside to peer out.

Paris lay below her. The pearly shades of early morning were spread like a film of finest chiffon over the still-sleeping city. Steep, slated roofs gleamed a dark grey-blue through the faint mist. In the distance, high on its hill, she could see the graceful minarets of the church of

Sacre Coeur, marble white against the tender blue of the sky. Below, the ribbon of the Seine wove its way through the city. Down there, amongst the streets, she knew that people were already beginning to stir, to run out to the *boulangerie* for fresh bread. The streets were being washed with the streams of water that ran every morning in the gutters. Paris was waking up.

And so, soon, would James. And she knew that she couldn't face him.

Moving silently across the carpet, she opened the bedroom door with a stealth that would have done credit to a cat burglar. Slowly, inch by inch, praying that James would be asleep, she pushed it ajar. She peeped round it and drew a breath of relief.

James lay under the tumbled sheet, sprawled across the bed, fast asleep. His dark hair was all that she could see of him, but when she came closer she could see the curve of his cheek, the lashes spread out like a black fan...

A momentary weakness shook her. Suppose she simply slid into bed beside him, pressed her body against his, wrapped her arms about him. Suppose she just *pretended* that everything was all right...

No. It would never work. What had happened last night would always lie between them.

And suppose James didn't *want* to pretend nothing had happened? Suppose he were really

146

in love with this fairy girl, this Ginette...

Still moving quietly, her fingers trembling, Rosalind picked up her bag and the clothes she had worn yesterday, which she had left draped across a chair. The dress James had bought for her to wear to the ballet, she left lying where he had dropped it last night. She could hardly bear to look at it; she would never wear it again.

As she reached the door, she paused for a last glance back. He was still in the same position, still asleep. Rosalind stared at him. For a moment, she felt an actual physical pain, as if something inside her were really breaking. Breaking slowly, agonisedly, breaking into a thousand tiny, jagged pieces. Oh, James, she thought, James ... Why, why did it have to happen ...?

And then, before she could weaken again, she slipped quickly out of the room and closed the door silently behind her.

She had dressed rapidly then, her fingers fumbling with the fastenings, terrified that he would wake and come to look for her. It seemed to take for ever before she was ready to leave, but at last she found herself outside the apartment, closing the door behind her. And she ran down the stairs and out into the street feeling as if she had escaped from something.

From a prison? From some sort of predator? She didn't know. But the feeling of release, mixed with the turmoil of bitter pain and grief, was enough to take her to the nearest taxi stand and then to the airport. And so to the first morning flight to London.

Her flight was called and she got up quickly, going through the departure lounge without glancing back. Already, France lay behind her. And ahead was—what? London, her job, her mother in the Cotswolds. A life to go back to, but a life that seemed empty now, without meaning. A life that without James, seemed hardly worth living.

She boarded the plane mechanically, found her seat, sat gazing unseeingly out of the window. She fastened the seat belt across her lap, watched without interest as the plane began to taxi, felt the lift and saw the ground drop away beneath them. She looked down at the map of France unfolding beneath her, saw the shining roofs of Paris in the distance, thought of the busy life that was teeming in its narrow streets, along its boulevards.

Somewhere down there, James was stirring under his sheet, perhaps reaching out for her—but why for her? Perhaps it was some other woman he felt for, expected to find in his bed.

But he would remember, she thought sadly. He would remember the loving they had shared last night, the loving that had seemed so real, so true. He would remember the phone call, the brief, bitter quarrel, the way Rosalind had left him.

And he would get up and look for her. He

would go into each room in the flat, searching, calling her name. And then he would see that she had taken her clothes and her bag, and he would understand.

And then? Would he follow her to London, intent on saving his marriage, realising at last what he was throwing away?

Or would he simply shrug and tidy up the scattered bedclothes, hang up the discarded dress and go off to his office?

And make his first phone call of the day—to Ginette...

$*$　　$*$　　$*$

'You're coming down again? This weekend?' Sheila sounded surprised and almost, Rosalind thought with disquiet, disconcerted. 'Well, I *am* getting a lot of attention lately, aren't I? They do say it's an ill wind that blows nobody any good. This trip of James's to Paris does at least mean I get to see more of my daughter.'

Rosalind closed her eyes, translating this as: '*You never came to see me enough, but now that you haven't got James to occupy you, I'm good enough as second best.*' Or was she being unfair? Did her mother deliberately barb every word she uttered, or could she just not help it because she really was lonely, because she really did miss her only child?

Guiltily, she said, 'So it'll be all right if I come on Friday then?'

'Well, yes, I suppose so.' Again that faint, inexplicable note of reluctance. 'But I'll have to warn you that I shall be out for most of Saturday. I'm going to an Antiques Fair in Moreton-in-the-Marsh.'

'Well, that's all right. I'll come with you.'

'Well, that's just it, darling. You know there's nothing I'd like better, but I've already arranged to go with Richard. And then we're having dinner in Broadway and I think it's too late to add on another person. So you see—'

'It's quite all right, Mother.' Rosalind couldn't help the chill creeping into her voice. Didn't her mother realise she was desperate, needed help, someone to talk to? 'I'm a big girl now, I can amuse myself.' But she had never felt less like a big girl, she thought miserably. Never felt more like a child, needing the comfort of its mother's arms ... 'We can spend Sunday together, I suppose.'

'Oh yes, that's all right.' Sheila sounded relieved. 'I've nothing arranged for Sunday.'

Rosalind put down the phone. She felt bleak, as if she had just been deserted by someone she had always relied on. Doubly deserted, she thought, remembering James's betrayal. And she made a sudden, sharp movement, as if trying to twist away from the grief that poured into her whenever she thought of James.

But there was no escape. This was a pain that came with her wherever she went, always there

150

in her heart, nagging quietly, ready to leap with unsheathed claws should she be unwary enough to let the thoughts take shape.

She tried not to, tried to keep them at bay, tried to think of other things. But she always returned to it, as a prying tongue will return to an aching tooth, to see if it really did hurt as much as memory insisted. To prove that it was still there.

Would she really talk to her mother about this? Would she really confide in her, tell her the intimate secrets of her marriage, ask her advice?

Rosalind tried to remember when she had last confided in her mother about something that really mattered, and found that she couldn't. Oh, she'd tried once or twice in her early teens, but Sheila had never quite responded in the way that Rosalind had wanted. She'd dismissed worries about boys, wrapping Rosalind in her arms and declaring that it was too soon to be thinking of such things, that a girl's mother should be the most important figure in her life, that there would be plenty of time for that later on. She hadn't wanted to know. It was as if even then she had been afraid that Rosalind was going to leave her.

And that fear had never lessened. As Rosalind had grown older, she had learned not to tell her mother if she was going out with a boy. There would always be some reason why she shouldn't. He wasn't a reliable boy, she knew of his reputation, he wasn't the sort of boy Sheila wanted her daughter to be seen with, he wasn't 'their sort'. Or maybe he was too old, too sophisticated; Rosalind should stay with friends of her own age.

Always something. And it hadn't been until Rosalind went away to college to study design that she had really begun to make friendships, to feel free to experiment.

Not that she'd experimented for long. In her second term, she had met James, then a young lecturer, and from then on they'd been inseparable. By the time Rosalind had finished her course they were engaged, and when they both applied for and got jobs with Lords & Ladies, they had married.

Sheila had liked James, Rosalind knew that. In fact, she had seen in her mother's eyes an interest that went beyond mere liking, and she'd been the one then to feel jealous. But it hadn't lasted. She felt too protective of Sheila to allow such a destructive emotion to come between them.

Confident now, sure of herself, she'd seen her mother through different eyes. She'd seen herself as the strong one, looking after her mother, keeping her from unpleasantness, keeping her happy. And although she'd often felt impatient, often chafed at the cords that still seemed to bind them—cords Sheila would never cut, always wanting to know where

Rosalind was, what she was doing, wanting frequent phone calls and regular visits—she'd never expressed that impatience.

'Mother only has me,' she would say to James. 'I can't let her down.' And so they would go down for another weekend, even though Rosalind knew she would return feeling irritated and confined by her mother's possessiveness, her clinging ways. But that, she told herself, was just part of the price one pays for having a loving mother. And that being so, she would pay it. Willingly.

But now, now that she was in real trouble, she wanted the positions reversed again. She wanted the comfort of a mother who understood, who would take her in warm arms and soothe her, tell her that it didn't matter, everything would be all right. Who would *make* things right.

Could Sheila do that, as she had done when Rosalind was fourteen and sobbing over the slight dealt her by some boy?

Could she make everything right again between her and James? Even though Rosalind herself was bitterly certain that it could never be the same again?

CHAPTER EIGHT

'Why didn't you let me know you were coming?' Troy Ballard leaned negligently against the kitchen door, smiling the slow, curving smile that gradually revealed his perfect white teeth.

He watched as Rosalind poured two mugs of coffee and then took the tray from her and walked through to the sitting room. 'Here all right?'

She nodded, and he set the tray down on a small table. Then he dropped gracefully on to the sofa and cocked one eyebrow at her. 'Come and sit beside me.' He patted the seat beside him.

Rosalind hesitated slightly, then sat down, slightly apart from him, and Troy smiled and laid his arm across the back of the sofa. He leaned back into the corner and regarded her quizzically. 'We're seeing a lot of you down here lately. And very nice too. Finding it a little lonely in London, now that your husband's away?'

'Not really.' Rosalind spoke defensively. She hadn't been at all sure how she felt about meeting Troy again. Their last meeting and what had almost happened was still very much in her mind and she felt an uneasy guilt, as if she really had been unfaithful to James.

But I wasn't, she argued, and I wouldn't have been. Even if Lisa hadn't phoned when she did, I would have drawn back. Of course I would.

All the same, she wasn't sure it was wise to be alone with him, certainly not so soon. And she'd been disconcerted when he arrived on the doorstep, not long after Sheila and the Brigadier had departed for their Antiques Fair.

'Did you know I'd be here?' she asked now, cradling her coffee mug in her hands. The warmth of it seeped through to her fingers.

Troy opened his eyes wide and shook his head. 'Now how would I have known that? You didn't let me know. Although I hope you wouldn't have gone away again without getting in touch.'

'Well, there were one or two things I wanted to discuss about the cottage,' she murmured, and he laughed.

'Well, that's good! What would I do without the cottage to keep us together? And is that the only reason you might have given me a ring, or come over to see me, Rosalind?'

She looked up, met his eyes and felt her skin warm in a deep blush. 'No, it isn't,' she said in a low voice. 'I would have wanted to see you because—because you're a friend.'

'And quite right too,' he said firmly. 'What better reason could there be? That's it, Rosalind—we're friends. And always will be, I hope.'

He made no move to touch her, and she met his eyes and saw the frankness in them, and felt reassured. He meant what he said. He was her friend—nothing more. No doubt he felt as thankful as she that a potentially dangerous situation had been defused the previous week, and wanted to set their relationship on a footing they both understood.

'Friends,' he said quietly, and held out his hand.

Rosalind took it. The long fingers curled around hers and she felt a tremor, but pushed it resolutely away. No more of that, she told herself. Things are complicated enough as it is. 'Friends,' she said.

They held hands for a moment longer, then Troy released her fingers and leaned forward to pick up his coffee. He began to talk about the village, how much he was enjoying getting to know people here, how he was looking forward to settling in the cottage. The main building work was almost completed now, he said, and they would soon be able to start on the more interesting work inside.

He was eager to see the new ideas and plans Rosalind had, and she got up and went to her bedroom to fetch them down. She spread them on the table and together they pored over them.

'Yes, I like these ideas very much,' Troy said at last. 'It's going to look exactly as I wanted. You and I obviously have the same ideas about how a home should be, Rosalind.'

Startled, Rosalind looked at the plans. There could be nothing more different from her own flat in London, she thought. This was an old cottage, furnished in an appropriate style, and the flat she had decorated with James was ultra-modern, full of white light and high-tech furniture. Perhaps Troy thought it was all James's taste. And yet, although she had had as much say in the decor as James, she was beginning to wonder if she really did like it after all. If she really felt at home in it.

She looked around her mother's sitting room. Also furnished in a style appropriate to the building itself, it was perfect—yet was it just a shade too perfect? Did she ever feel absolutely at home here? Or did she feel slightly guilty, as if by sitting in the chairs or putting a coffee mug on the table, she was spoiling its careful symmetry, its conscious charm?

She cast around in her mind for a place where she really did feel at home. And found herself thinking of James's parents' house. Plain, shabby, haphazardly furnished and decorated by bits and pieces they had collected around them on what his mother had called her 'journey through life'—yet unmistakably a home, where a family was glad to gather together, where newspapers were dropped on chairs, cats curled in patches of sunlight, children's toys were scattered perilously about the floor...

'Is something worrying you, Rosalind?' Troy asked, and the sudden gentleness of his tone brought unexpected tears to her eyes.

'No—of course not. Nothing at all. I was just thinking about homes—yours and mine, how different they are. That sort of thing.'

'Ah yes, but they're different kinds of place, aren't they? These ideas you're suggesting for my cottage wouldn't do at all in your smart London flat. Just as high-tech furniture would look ridiculous in a house like this. But you know that—you don't need me to teach you your job.' He paused, then added in the same quiet tone, 'All the same, I get the feeling there is something wrong, Rosalind. And you know what I told you before—if you ever need a listener, a shoulder to cry on...'

'I know. And I'm grateful, Troy. But it's just something I've got to sort out for myself.' She realised that she hadn't denied, this time, that there was something. She looked up and met his eyes. Suppose she did tell him—what would his reaction be? Would he take her in his arms, let her literally cry on his shoulder? Would he comfort her, soothe her, take care of her?

Would he lay his lips on her hair, move his long, sensitive fingers over her cheek, her neck ... and would he begin to love her?

She was shaken by a sudden almost overwhelming desire to go to his arms, to let him do all those things, to take the comfort she knew he could give her. The comfort she so desperately needed.

But the thought of James held her back. James, her husband, who had betrayed her and yet whom she still loved. I can't stop loving him, she thought miserably, and turned her head away from Troy's gaze. I can't just turn it off like a tap, whatever he's done. And I can't go to another man's arms in revenge. Or even just to look for comfort.

'Just talk about it, if you like,' Troy said softly, but she shook her head.

'No. I'm not ready to talk—yet. Maybe later—I don't know. Maybe there's nothing to talk about anyway.' She bit back the tears and lifted her head, then turned and smiled into his eyes. 'I'll tell you what I'd like to do, if you're offering. Go and have a pub lunch somewhere and then walk. It's such a beautiful day, much too good to spend indoors, and the woods will be full of spring flowers. And I seem to have spent all my time this week either in offices or travelling between them.'

And in Paris. On planes going to and from Paris. In restaurants in Paris. At the ballet in Paris. And in James's apartment—in Paris.

She needed to push all that away, out of her mind, set as much space and time as she could between herself and the memories. Maybe then she'd be able to take them out again and look at them without this awful, jagged pain. Maybe then she'd know what she had to do.

*   *   *

Sheila and the Brigadier did not return until after ten o'clock that evening and Rosalind, hearing the Brigadier's car draw up outside, met them at the door. Since Troy had left her, after a cup of tea when they'd returned from their lunch and walk, she had been alone in the cottage. She had sat listlessly turning over the pages of magazines, switching on the TV, playing records, but nothing had served to hold her attention. Several times she had looked at the telephone, wondering whether to call James. But what would be the use? He was almost certain to be out—and probably with Ginette, she thought bitterly. And if he were in, what could they say to each other? Especially as she knew she would be equally certain that Ginette was in the flat with him.

No, she could not ring James.

She thought a little resentfully of how Troy, having taken her out to a village about fifteen miles away for a delicious lunch and then enjoyed a couple of hours walking with her through woods strewn with primroses and violets, the trees bursting into leaf all around them, had brought her back home with the regretful but firm announcement that he could not spend the evening with her, since he already had a prior engagement.

'Some old friends of mine who live near Stow,' he'd explained. 'And Susan's rather particular about her dinner-parties—matches all the guests carefully, must have the right number at the table and so on. Otherwise I'd take you along. But as it is...'

'Oh, I wouldn't dream of gate-crashing,' Rosalind had said at once, and she'd waved him off with a bright smile pinned to her face. And gone back indoors feeling suddenly bereft. Left out of everything. Left out of life.

But it was no use being sorry for herself, and she'd tried hard to fill in the hours until her mother came home.

All the same, she was thankful when they did finally come home and fill the house with life again.

'Hallo, darling.' Sheila swept into the room, unwinding silk scarves from around her neck, dropping gloves and bag on a side table, casting a glance around, almost as if to assure herself that nothing had been moved during her absence. 'Have you been very lonely? We would have come back earlier, but the restaurant was so good, you couldn't hurry the meal. And then we stopped on Broadway Hill and looked at the moon ... Quite romantic!' She laughed a little self-consciously, glancing sideways at the Brigadier, and Rosalind felt a spasm of irritation. Was her mother going into some sort of second childhood?

'Sounds lovely,' she said coolly. 'No, I haven't been lonely at all. Troy dropped in this morning—he brought you a book he said you wanted—and we went out to lunch and then walked through the woods. And since then I've had a lovely quiet evening all to myself. Quite a treat, really.'

'A treat? But I thought you were complaining that you had too many quiet evenings these days.' Sheila spoke almost absently, as if she wasn't really paying much attention to her own words. She had dropped into an armchair beside the fire and leant forward to poke the smouldering logs into flame. Then she jumped up again. 'I'll make some coffee. You two can have a chat while I'm in the kitchen.'

Somewhat annoyed by her mother's tactlessness, Rosalind glanced up and caught the Brigadier's eyes on her face. She turned away abruptly.

'I'm sorry we couldn't take you with us today,' he said after a moment. 'A pity for you to come all this way and have to spend the day alone.'

'I've already said, it was perfectly pleasant.' She knew that her voice was too tight for politeness and made an effort to relax. 'I always enjoy coming home for the weekend. And Troy is good company and we've quite a lot to talk about.'

'Ye-es,' he said thoughtfully. 'But not a substitute for your husband, I fear.'

'What do you mean? I'm not looking for a substitute for James—'

He shook his head at once. 'I know that, my dear. Your mother has told me how close you two are, how happy you've been together.'

How happy we've *been*? she thought. What had her mother been saying?

'There's nothing that can take the place of a loved companion—the one person who can walk with you through life, sharing the good and the bad times, the walks through the woods, the evenings by the fire...' He stopped and smiled at her, rather sadly, she thought. 'And when you've had that joy and then lost it—'

'Lost it?' she echoed blankly. What *had* her mother been saying? What did she know? 'But I haven't—'

'No—no, of course not. I wasn't speaking personally in any way, you realise.' He reached over and patted her hand. 'Just letting you know that we do understand how lonely you must feel, with James away so much. And you know, don't you, that you're only too welcome to come down whenever you want to— whenever you need a little company. Your mother and I—' He stopped as Sheila returned, bearing a tray of cups.

She looked at him, her brows raised a little. 'And what's this about us? You're not telling my daughter any secrets, I hope?'

He laughed. 'Not a single secret has passed my lips, I assure you. Rosalind was just telling me how much she enjoys coming home.'

163

'That's all right, then.' Sheila smiled at him, a warm, almost conspiratorial smile. She turned to Rosalind. 'And how nice to hear you call it home. It's so long since you've lived here. I would have thought you'd have stopped thinking of this little cottage in that way.'

Rosalind felt hurt. 'Of course I haven't! This will always be home to me.' She looked around, feeling a sudden affection for the old walls, the uneven floors that no amount of designer decor could conceal. 'It's special.'

Sheila handed Richard his coffee. She seemed to hesitate, as if about to speak, then changed her mind. Instead, she sat down in one of the big armchairs, looking small as a child in its depths, and stretched her arms above her head. 'Well, let's hope you always will remember it that way,' she said lightly. 'Everyone should have happy memories of home, and I did always try to give you those. It's nice to think I might have succeeded.'

Rosalind took the other chair, leaving Richard alone on the sofa. 'Of course you succeeded. Why do you suppose I keep coming back?'

But there was something in what her mother had said—or in the tone in which she'd said it—or perhaps even in what she had *not* said—that made her feel slightly uneasy. And it wasn't long before she yawned and, making an excuse about country air, declared that she was tired and going to bed.

'Good-night, Richard,' she said politely and then, bending to kiss Sheila, 'Night, Mother. See you in the morning. And we'll have a lovely, lazy day together doing absolutely nothing, shall we?'

'Sounds delicious, darling.' Sheila's cheek was smooth and faintly scented. 'Sleep as late as you like. I'll be around.'

Rosalind turned at the door and looked back at them. They looked cosy and domestic together, her mother and the Brigadier. Almost Darby and Joanish.

She felt another little pang of unease. Surely ... But no. It was a ridiculous idea. Crazy. Her mother had too much sense.

But as she climbed the stairs to the bedroom that had been hers ever since she was a child, her thoughts went back to her own troubles.

James. James and herself. James and Ginette...

The one person who can walk with you through life ... The Brigadier's words came back to her like a douche of icy water. The loved companion. The walks through the woods. The evenings by the fire.

We've never had that kind of companionship, James and I, she thought bleakly. We've only ever had a working relationship. We've only ever shared our working lives—our careers. All our discussions have been about other people's homes, about someone else's sofas, someone else's dining room. Someone else's bed ...

But that's not true, another part of her argued. We designed our flat together, we chose the colour scheme and the furniture, shared the decorating. We made our own home.

She closed the bedroom door and leaned against it, looking round at the dainty, flowery wallpaper she had chosen herself, the sprigged curtains, the soft patchwork quilt she had inherited from her grandmother. With a slight shock, she realised that nothing had been changed in this room since it had been redecorated for her fourteenth birthday. No matter how smart and "country-chic" her mother had made the rest of the cottage, this room had always been kept the same. Slightly shabby, but familiar, and comfortable in that familiarity.

No, she thought, we didn't make a home. We made a showplace. A place we could bring people to and without saying a word, impress them with our taste and our talents. *This* is a home.

And as she crossed the room to draw the curtains she had always loved, yet which would have looked totally out of place in the smart white London flat, she felt a sudden desolation. Is that all that James and I have to share? she wondered. An interest in interior design? A career?

No wonder it had all begun to fall apart. No

wonder their marriage could not survive the rupture of that sole common interest.

*   *   *

'Did you,' she asked her mother as they sat in the sun lounge next morning, finishing a late breakfast, 'feel very lonely after my father died?'

Sheila poured the last of the coffee and sat back, considering. 'What a funny question. Of course I felt lonely. I was very young, after all—not much more than a bride. But I had you, and you were *such* a comfort to me. I often thought I might have gone mad if I hadn't had my darling baby daughter to work for and keep me company.' She leaned over and touched Rosalind's hand. 'And you always were a comfort to me, darling. All through your baby days, your childhood, even into those terrible teens! I never wanted anyone else as long as I had you.'

Rosalind stared at her, feeling a lump in her throat. She had never realised just how much she meant to her mother—never really given it any thought at all, other than to feel irritated at what she saw as the shackles of possessiveness. Now she saw her mother's feelings in a different light, as love, and herself as a reason for living.

Just as James was her reason for living, she thought with a sudden sickening lurch of her

167

heart. And she had lost him as surely as her mother had, long ago, lost her own husband, Rosalind's father.

'You must have felt lonely when I left, then,' she said slowly, feeling a guilt that was eight years in the past creep over her like a fog. 'When I went to college and never really came back. Because you must have known quite soon that I would marry James.'

'Oh yes, I did. I never saw any two young people more in love than you and James. But I knew you would leave me some day, and when I got to know James I knew he would never really take you away from me. Not that anyone would ever be able to do that,' she added with another pat on Rosalind's hand. 'We're far too close for anyone to come between us, aren't we? Much more like friends really, than mother and daughter.'

Rosalind looked at the small, soft hand covering her own. She felt tears come hot into her eyes and blinked them quickly away.

More like friends than mother and daughter. But we *are* mother and daughter, she wanted to cry. It's a special relationship—far, far more than friendship. Don't let's deny it, don't let's pretend it doesn't exist.

And then: if we are such good friends, so close, why can't I talk to you about James? Why can't I tell you what's happening in my life? Why do I have to go on trying to protect you, trying to pretend that everything's perfect, like some TV ad of the ideal young couple? Why can't I be *honest* with you?

Why can't I ask for the comfort I need so much?

There could be only one reason, she thought as she made some excuse to leave the table and went up to her room before Sheila could see the tears. It could only be because she and her mother weren't really as close as they liked to pretend. Because they were walking on a thin veneer of pretence, and both were afraid to crack it by telling each other the truth.

*   *   *

They spent the rest of the morning unpacking some of the pieces that Sheila had bought yesterday at the Antiques Fair, cataloguing them and setting them out in the shop. It was pleasant enough work and gave them something to do together without having to talk. Rosalind felt a painful sadness that they had been reduced to this—a displacement activity, she supposed psychologists would call it, like a cat washing itself when it didn't want to acknowledge a rival. But there was no rivalry between her and Sheila, was there? So just what was this barrier that seemed to have risen between them?

Somehow, it seemed to be closely tied up with the barrier between herself and James, yet she could not see why, could find no connection. And there was certainly no one she could talk to about it.

Unless...

She thought of Troy Ballard, his gentleness, his offer to be a listener, a shoulder to cry on. And she felt a sudden longing to be with him, to pour out all her troubles, to be taken in those strong arms, stroked with those sensitive hands, to be soothed and looked after and made better...

'This is a nice piece,' Sheila remarked, lifting a graceful Georgian candelabra from the packing case that stood between them. 'You know, I didn't expect to find much to buy yesterday but there was quite a lot. We were there early, of course. But it's surprising what turns up at some of these amateur Fairs.'

'It was a charity thing, wasn't it?' Rosalind wasn't really interested, but it was better than letting her thoughts circle so endlessly about the same insoluble problems.

'Mm. All the local charities get together a couple of times a year and book the local hall. They run a stall each. One in spring and one just before Christmas. And since they collect stuff that people throw out of their attics, without any idea as to what it's worth, it's possible to pick up some quite good pieces. I was surprised to find this, though.' Sheila was polishing the candelabra and she stood it on a small desk and admired it. 'Whoever owned that could have got quite a decent price in an antique shop.'

'Such as yours,' Rosalind suggested with a smile.

'Certainly. I'd have paid more than I did yesterday for that and still expected to make a profit. It seems silly to me. They could have brought it to me, got a better price, and donated that to their charity. Still, I'm not complaining. It makes me a living!' She gave the candelabra a final rub and carried it across to the window. 'I'll put it here. It'll attract the eye nicely.'

There was a short silence. Rosalind unpacked a porcelain figure that she was nearly sure was Dresden, and was just about to ask her mother's opinion when Sheila, still at the window, spoke again.

'I'm glad you came down this weekend, Rosalind. There's something I've been wanting to ask you, but—well, the time wasn't quite right. Now, I think it is. Only—' she gave a little, nervous laugh, '—I'm not quite sure how to say it.'

Rosalind gazed at her. Her heart jumped a little. So her mother had noticed after all that there was something wrong.

She waited for the inevitable question, not quite sure even now how to answer it. Should she go on pretending, protecting her mother's peace of mind, keeping up the facade of a happy marriage? Or should she do what she longed to do—pour it all out, all the loneliness,

171

the growing suspicion, the heartache, and hand it all over to a mother who would know just what to do, how to offer comfort, how to make everything all right again? She set the little figure down carefully and waited, her breath coming quickly.

But when Sheila began to speak, it was as if she had forgotten what she was about to say and gone off completely at a tangent. It was as if she had forgotten about Rosalind herself. And it was a moment or two before Rosalind could focus her attention on the words and make any sense of them at all.

'You must have noticed something,' Sheila was saying, blushing and half-smiling like a schoolgirl. 'I mean, he's been here several times now, you know we've been seeing quite a lot of each other. It can't come as much of a surprise. So I thought—well, what's the point in keeping it a secret? Everyone's going to know soon enough, anyway. And Richard—well, he suggested you might like to—to give me away.'

'*Give you away?*' Rosalind stared at her mother. 'Mother, what on earth are you talking about?'

'Richard and me, of course.' Sheila looked faintly aggrieved. 'Haven't you been listening? I've just told you, we're getting married. Not just yet, of course, there's a lot to arrange, but on the other hand we're neither of us of an age for a long engagement. And I thought I'd better warn you so that you and James can keep your time free for the wedding and—'

'*Wedding?* You and—and the Brigadier?' Rosalind could almost feel her brain struggling to change gear. 'I'm dreaming,' she said flatly. 'This conversation isn't happening. I'm asleep. I'll wake up in a minute and everything will be normal again. I—'

'Rosalind, stop it!' Sheila said sharply. 'What do you mean, everything will be normal? It's normal now. What's so strange about two people deciding they're sufficiently fond of each other to get married? Or do you think we're too old to be thinking of such things?'

Rosalind gazed at her. She wanted to say yes, that's exactly what I do think, but she managed to hold on to her senses and keep the words back. However, she could not help saying that while her mother was certainly not too old, the Brigadier was surely—well . . .

'He's sixty-two,' Sheila said forthrightly. 'Not exactly in his dotage, though I can see that he must seem so to you. Ten years older than I am. Not much more of a gap than there is between you and James. And he's not marrying me for my money, such as it is—he's very comfortably off. So what exactly is worrying you, Rosalind?'

Rosalind shook her head. The news had come as such a complete shock to her that she hadn't even begun to sort out her feelings about it. She only knew that she didn't like it.

173

That there was something wrong, very wrong indeed, in the idea of her mother marrying the Brigadier. But what it was, she hadn't yet had time to analyse.

'And I wish you'd stop calling him *the Brigadier*, as if he were a toy soldier,' Sheila said crisply. 'His name is Richard and since he'd going to be your stepfather, you'd better get used to it.'

She paused for a moment, then went on in a softer tone, 'I can see this has come as a surprise to you, Rosalind, and you're going to need a little time to come to terms with it. But I'm sure, when you've had time to think it over, you'll be glad for me. After all, you can't want me to go on for the rest of my life being lonely. Especially now you've left me.'

'But you haven't lost me!' Rosalind cried. 'I'm still your daughter. You're still special to me. Oh, I know we irritate each other sometimes but that's natural, surely. We love each other, really—and you'll never lose me, never.'

It was the most emotional speech she had ever made to her mother and she expected Sheila to dissolve into tears, but instead her mother just smiled calmly and came away from the shop window to pat Rosalind's arm.

'That's a lovely thing to say,' she said gently. 'But you know perfectly well that it's true only up to a point. You have your own life to lead now, with James, and you've been leading it for several years. You can't expect me to mark time just waiting for your visits. I'm still comparatively young, and I want to live too. And I want to live with Richard.'

Live with Richard ... The words had a peculiarly distasteful connotation when applied to her mother. Rosalind shook her head and moved away. She knew that she ought to say something congratulatory, murmur something about wishing them both happiness, express her pleasure at the news ... but the words would not come. The feeling that had begun to grown in her, that her relationship with Sheila was based on a kind of dishonesty, would not let her tell the conventional lies. She didn't want to congratulate her mother. She didn't want to wish them happiness, or say how pleased she was. Because none of it was true, and Sheila would know it wasn't true.

'Excuse me,' she said, turning to the door. 'I just have to go upstairs—something I forgot to do ...' And somehow, blindly, she made her escape and stumbled out of the shop, back into the cottage and up to her room. And there, surrounded by the mementoes of her childhood, she sank down on the bed and cried. She cried for her mother. She cried for her lost childhood. She cried for the mess her life seemed to be in, for the sense that she had no one to turn to, that everything was going wrong around her.

And she cried for herself.

*   *   *

'James,' she said, 'James. Oh, James...' She was back in the flat. She had picked up the telephone the moment she came through the door. For a short time all the fear, all the tension between them, had been swept away in an overpowering need to hear her husband's voice.

'Rosalind?' he said, and even though he was several hundred miles away, his voice was guarded, wary. 'Is that you?'

'Of course it's me!' They might not have spoken to each other since that terrible night when Ginette had telephoned him and Rosalind had realised the extent of the danger her marriage was in, but he surely couldn't have forgotten the sound of her voice ... 'James, I must talk to you. I've just been down to Mother's—'

'There's nothing wrong, is there?' His voice had sharpened. 'Sheila's all right?'

'Yes—at least, she's all right in the sense you mean. She's not ill or anything.' Rosalind felt a pang of disappointment that he had not asked how she was herself. His concern was, it seemed, all for her mother. 'James—'

'Yes?' He sounded slightly impatient now. 'What is it, Rosalind? What's the matter?'

Can't I just ring you to say hello? she

thought miserably. Does there have to be something the matter? But at least he was talking to her. After the way she'd left him, she wouldn't have been surprised if he'd simply put down the phone when he heard her voice.

'It's Mother,' she said a little dully. And then, 'James, that man was there again. That Brigadier—Richard. They went out together—to an antiques fair in Moreton-in-the-Marsh, and then they had dinner in some romantic little restaurant on the way home. And—'

'It all sounds very pleasant,' he said remotely. 'And did you go along too?'

'No. No. Mother didn't invite me. They didn't want me with them, James.' To her intense annoyance, she felt the tears pricking her eyelids. I sound like a spoilt child, she thought, and strove to bring a more adult, indifferent tone to her voice. 'Not that I wanted to go, actually. I had a very pleasant day. I went out to lunch with—with a friend, and we had a walk in the woods and then I spent the evening reading and watching TV.'

'So why are you ringing me up to tell me about it? I take it that is what you wanted to tell me about? There wasn't anything else you wanted to discuss? Anything more important, perhaps?'

'But this *is* important!' she cried. 'James, they're talking about getting married. Mother and the Brigadier. She told me about it yesterday, while we were unpacking the things they'd bought. They want to get *married*, James.'

There was a long pause. Then he said with an odd note in his voice, 'Well, well, well.'

'Is that all you can say?' Rosalind felt a familiar sense of frustration. 'Don't you understand what it means? She'll be *living* with him—in the same house. They'll always be together—'

'Yes, I know what marriage means,' he broke in quietly. 'Or at least, I thought I did. I'm glad to find that the dear old institution is still alive and kicking in some places.'

Rosalind bit her lip. 'There's no need to be sarcastic. It was you who went away—'

'For a very short time. For six months. Not for a lifetime and not to the end of the world. You were free to come over any time you like. I would have welcomed your company.'

'That's not the impression I got,' Rosalind retorted. 'You never once mentioned my coming over to Paris. It was always you coming back to London—if you had the time. And it doesn't seem as it you have, very often.'

'No,' he said, 'I don't. So when I'm tied up for Saturday, you could have come over here, couldn't you? Spent the day sightseeing or shopping or whatever else took your fancy, and then we could have had the evening and Sunday together. What would have been wrong with that? And when I do have the whole weekend, I like to come home. The place I used to think of as home, anyway,' he added with a touch of bitterness.

Rosalind felt as if the breath had been knocked out of her body. 'Why didn't you ever suggest I come to Paris?' she demanded. 'It wouldn't have been hard to say, would it? If you'd really wanted me—'

'Why didn't *you* suggest it? If *you'd* really wanted *me!*'

The all too familiar exasperation swept over her once more. Of course she'd wanted him. She couldn't have made it any plainer. And if only he'd said, just once—*come* to *Paris for the weekend, I'm missing you*—why, she'd have gone like a shot. She would have known he wanted her—and it would have meant the world to her.

But he never had.

'I'm sorry,' she said wearily. 'I can't cope with this. James, all I rang up about was to tell you about Mother. I never meant to start an argument—'

'So,' he said in the polite, remote voice she hated the most, 'you've told me. Was there anything else?'

Rosalind clutched the telephone receiver as if she were strangling it. 'Anything else? Isn't that enough?'

'I've no idea,' he said, still in that hateful voice. 'You tell me.'

Rosalind took a deep breath. 'James, I'd just

like to talk about it. You know what Mother's like. I just wanted to—to—'

'To hear me say how terrible it is?' he asked. 'But I don't see that it is.' His voice had relaxed a little. Perhaps this was the right approach, to get him talking impersonally, to keep off their own affairs. 'He seems a decent enough guy to me.'

'Well, yes, I'm not saying he's not. It's just...' She paused. James wasn't reacting as she wanted him to, and she tried to put into words her feelings of—what? What exactly were her feelings? Even after the drive back to London, with her thoughts racing in her brain, she still hadn't quite sorted out what she didn't like about this engagement. Shock—yes. But what else? Distaste? Betrayal? She veered away from such ideas. 'I just want what's best for Mother,' she said at last. 'And I'm not at all sure that this is.'

'But how would you know?' James enquired reasonably. 'You've always thought of Sheila as your mother—full stop. You've never seen her as a woman, with her own needs. Maybe she's been desperately lonely all these years, waiting for the right man to come along. And now he has. What's wrong with that?'

Rosalind rejected the thought that Sheila had been desperately lonely. She'd had Rosalind, hadn't she? She'd said so, only this morning at breakfast. This morning! It seemed like years ago.

'Nothing's wrong with it,' she admitted, 'if he *is* the right man for Mother. But I'm not sure he is. I think she might be making a dreadful mistake.'

'Well, that's her privilege.' James was beginning to sound bored again. 'Rosalind, you've got to stop clinging on to your mother. Let her live her own life, even if that means letting her make her own mistakes. Stop treating her like your child, and stop wanting her to treat you like hers.'

'But I *am* her child!' Rosalind was outraged. 'And I *don't* treat her like one. You don't understand at all. I love her—I don't want to see this man, this—this Brigadier—make her unhappy. I *worry* about her, James.'

'Well, stop it,' he said tersely. 'She doesn't want you to worry about her, any more than you've liked having her worry about you over the past few years. How often have you grumbled to me about her trying to keep you tied to her apron strings? Now she's let the strings go and decided to live her own life, you don't like that either. Look, she knows this man and you don't. She's old enough to know whether he's right for her or not. Let her go and stop acting like a dog in the manger.'

There was a brief silence. Then Rosalind said coldly, 'I might have known better than to expect any sympathy from you. I knew you wouldn't care how I felt, but I did think you were quite fond of my mother—'

'I am, for heaven's sake!'

'Well, it doesn't seem like it to me,' she flared. 'You don't really care about either of us, do you? You've left us behind. You're living a new life now, over there in France and we're just an irritating encumbrance. I daresay you're making plans to rid yourself of the burden even now—you and that little fairy doll you've taken up with!'

The silence this time could almost be felt. Then James, his voice like ice, said, 'And I suppose that's why you ran away the other morning. You were too scared to stay and face up to what you thought was the truth. You ran away and straight home to Mummy, and when she didn't want to know because she has her own life to lead, you've come whining back to me for sympathy over that. Do you know what you are, Rosalind? You're a child who has never grown up. Your body grew up, your mental capacity grew up, but emotionally you're still in your pram!'

Rosalind gasped. Then she slammed down the receiver, so hard that it cracked the rest and a piece of hard plastic shell flew on to the carpet. With a sob that seemed to tear her heart from her breast, she bent to pick it up.

The phone rang again, almost as soon as she had slammed it down. She picked it up, expecting to hear James's voice, expecting an apology.

'Oh, hi there, Rosalind,' said Troy Ballard's

voice, slow and warm as ever. 'You must have been sitting right on top of the phone ... Listen, I'm coming up to Town again this week and I wondered if we might repeat that very pleasant little exercise of dinner and a show? Say Tuesday evening? Do say yes...'

Rosalind held the receiver close against her ear. She stared at the white wall, thought of Troy Ballard here again, thought of the evening they'd spent together, the fun they'd had, the feeling that she could say anything to this man and he would understand.

She thought of his offer to be her listener, her shoulder to cry on. She thought of his kiss, here in this very flat. The feelings that had welled up in her at the touch of his hand.

'Rosalind? Are you still there? We haven't been cut off?'

'No,' she said. 'No, we haven't been cut off. And yes, I'd like that very much. Tuesday evening. Will you pick me up at about the same time?'

'I thought so.' There was a crinkle of amusement in his voice. 'And yes, I'll arrive around the same time. Especially if you promise to be wearing that very sexy little bath towel again ... See you on Tuesday, then, Rosalind. I'm looking forward to it already.'

He hung up and Rosalind put the phone down again, more slowly this time. She got up and walked across the room to a mirror, staring into it. Her oval face looked back at her, pale in spite of the sunshine of the weekend, framed by her silky, ash-blonde hair.

'Yes,' she said aloud. 'I'm looking forward to it too, Troy.'

CHAPTER NINE

The hours between Sunday evening and Tuesday crept slowly past. It wasn't that she was desperate to see Troy—Rosalind would not allow herself to believe that—but more that she longed for contact with someone who saw her as a person who was good company, a person who was worth spending time with. With the defection of both James and her mother, Rosalind was beginning to wonder if anyone else at all saw her in that light.

Clearly, James wasn't missing her at all. She played their conversation over in her head time and time again, listening to every nuance of his voice. He talked as if we were in a committee meeting, she thought miserably. *I take it there's nothing further to discuss?'* ... *'Was there anything else?'* ...Oh, James. What's happened to us? Where has it all gone?

His accusation that she didn't care enough to join him in Paris had almost taken her breath away. Of course she cared! And she would have loved to go to Paris—it would have eased the pain of their separation, made it fun

... But he had never even hinted at it, he had given her to understand that if he didn't come to London it was because he was too busy. So what would have been the point?

And in any case, she'd always been afraid of what she would find. First, her suspicions—unfounded, she now realised—about Lisa. And then her only too well-founded suspicions, confirmed by that after-midnight telephone call, about Ginette.

Ginette. For the thousandth time, Rosalind pictured the French girl. So tiny she could almost have been a child, yet her figure was as voluptuous as that of the Venus de Milo. Hair of sheer, spun gold, framing a face as delicately translucent as porcelain. And as hard, Rosalind thought, remembering the china-blue eyes that had gazed without expression into hers. But you couldn't expect a man to see that.

She looked like the fairy that James liked to set on top of their Christmas tree. Ethereal, ready to be blown away on the faintest zephyr breeze—yet as sexy as only a French girl could be. And as predatory...

I shouldn't blame him, Rosalind thought desolately. Things were going wrong between us long before he went to Paris. And with a girl like that flinging herself at him—and her father in a position to further James's career as well—what man could resist?

But she knew that until now she would have

believed that James could resist. That the love between him and herself would have stood firm against any temptation.

And that, she told herself, is where you made your mistake, Rosalind. Better face up to it. Get real, as they say. There isn't a man alive who can resist temptation—and maybe not so many women either.

She thought of Troy again. Tuesday evening, drawing closer and closer. The theatre, dinner in some intimate restaurant, coffee afterwards back here in the flat. The touch of his lips, last time. The touch of his hand.

I shouldn't let it happen, she thought. I won't let it happen. But her heart beat a little faster, and the betraying tingle of desire began low down in her stomach, spreading over her body, burning its way down her arms and into the palms of her hands.

She looked at the telephone. I mustn't let it happen. I mustn't feel this way. I'll ring him and cancel the date. I'll tell him our relationship has to be purely business from now on. No more romantic twosomes. No more walks in the woods. No more offers of a shoulder to cry on...

But she knew that she needed that shoulder, more desperately than she needed anything else. And where else was she to find one?

*　　*　　*

'And now,' Troy said firmly, as Rosalind brought the coffee through, 'I'm not going to take no for an answer any more. I'm going to insist, Rosalind.'

She looked at him, startled. Not once during the entire evening had Troy made any move that might be construed as an advance towards her. He had called for her at seven, as arranged, made some complimentary remarks about her appearance, taken her down to his car and settled her in the passenger seat as though she were royalty.

They had sat beside each other in the theatre, alternately laughing, crying (in Rosalind's case, anyway) and humming along to the songs that were so well known to everyone.

They had gone to a small restaurant, filled with theatre people all talking at the tops of their voices, so that it was like one huge party, and they had eaten a supper that was if anything even more delicious than they had shared before.

And then he had brought her home.

He had made no reference at all to the kisses they had shared, nor to any that they might share in the future.

All the time, Rosalind had been aware of the electricity between them, the attraction that sparked almost visibly, as static will spark from a hairbrush. She had been conscious of his arm almost touching hers in the theatre, of his head close to hers as he bent to murmur something in her ear, of the chiselled lines of his face, his eyes as silver as stars in the darkness. And she had wondered, with a quickening heart, just what might happen when he came back to the flat and she invited him in for coffee.

But again, he had made no move. He hadn't even followed her to the kitchen.

So now was he telling her that he expected payment for the evening out?

Well, she supposed she should have expected it. Some people might even say she'd asked for it. And now she'd have to deal with it.

Resignedly, she sat down in one of the chairs, but Troy shook his head and laid his hand on the seat beside him.

'Come and sit here, Rosalind,' he said gently, 'and tell me what's upsetting you so much.'

Rosalind felt a moment of shame. Had she misjudged him after all? She hesitated for a moment.

'I'm not going to leap on you, you know,' he said with a slightly quizzical look. 'I just want to help. It's obvious something's wrong. I told you, if you want to talk—well, I'll listen and it's quite possible I'll understand. I may even have been there myself,' he added ruefully.

Rosalind gave him a glance of surprise. But before she could ask what he meant, he had patted the seat beside him again and she took a breath and then crossed the space between them and sank down on the sofa.

He slipped his arm around her shoulders and almost without thinking, as if she were coming home, she laid her head on his shoulder.

'That's better,' he said softly. 'Now, tell your Uncle Troy all about it. What's nasty old Life done to you?'

Rosalind laughed a little in spite of herself. 'Oh, not that much really. Nothing very terrible at all, when you consider what some people go through. And it's all very ordinary really. Just—well, people not turning out to be what you think, I suppose. Realising that a lot of your life is based on an illusion.' She caught her breath with a tiny sob. 'It—it's just a bit difficult to come to terms with.'

'It certainly is. And by "people", do you mean your husband?'

'James ... yes, I suppose I do. But it isn't just him.' She didn't feel quite ready, yet, to tell Troy about James's duplicity, about the fairy creature who had cast a spell on him in Paris. 'My mother told me something at the weekend that rather upset me too. And when I rang James and told him—well, he just didn't seem to understand how I felt.'

'So you feel he let you down. D'you want to tell me?'

Rosalind thought for a moment. 'Yes, I do,' she said slowly. 'You know everyone involved and yet you're not too close. You might be able

189

to see things more clearly than any of us.'

She settled more comfortably against his broad chest. 'It's quite simple really. Mother told me on Sunday morning. It seems that she and—' But it wasn't simple at all, she discovered. It wasn't nearly so easy to say as she'd expected. 'She and—and the Brigadier— you know him, don't you? Well, they've been seeing quite a lot of each other apparently and now they—they—'

'They're getting married.' He spoke the words coolly, unemotionally, as if they were no surprise to him, and Rosalind twisted to look up into his face.

'You *knew*?'

Troy laughed. 'The whole village knows! Oh, not officially—not a word's been said yet. But you know what villages are like, everyone else knows your business before you know it yourself, and the local grapevine has been buzzing with it for weeks. We're all just waiting for our invitations. Why,' he said in some surprise, 'you're not telling me you don't like the idea, are you? Don't you approve of the Brig?'

Rosalind sighed. Here was someone else who approved, who thought it was 'sweet' and 'romantic' when two elderly people acted like teenagers. Well, perhaps not elderly exactly— she could just imagine her mother's reaction to being called that—but certainly old enough to know better.

'No,' she said shortly, 'I don't approve of him. He's too smooth. Too charming. Too *nice*. Oh, all right, so it sounds funny—' as Troy put back his head and roared with laughter—'but if it were your mother getting swept off her feet by a regimental tie, you might feel differently about it. I mean, it's all very exciting and thrilling now and I daresay they both feel young again, but how is it going to be in a year or two when he's getting older and depending on Mother to look after him, and she's tied to an old man for perhaps another twenty years? Suppose he goes senile or has a stroke and needs constant attention? How's she going to feel then, having given up all her freedom and independence?'

'Much the same as you'd feel if it were your James when you get to that age, I imagine,' he said. 'She'll probably want to look after him and make him comfortable and bring as much as she can to his life. At least, that's if she loves him, which I presume is why they're getting married in the first place.'

Rosalind was silent. At last she said quietly, 'You don't understand, do you? Nobody seems to understand how I feel.'

'Perhaps,' Troy suggested, 'it's because you're not really making much effort to understand how other people feel.'

Rosalind sat up. She looked at him. He looked back, steadily, and then drew her head down to his chest again.

'Don't feel so persecuted, Rosalind,' he said. 'There really isn't any need. You've got so many people who love you. All you have to do is to let them live their own lives. It'll make them happy, and that will make you happy too. Can you understand that?'

'I *do* let them live their lives,' she said, her voice muffled against his shirt. 'But they just go off and leave me. James has gone to Paris and I don't know if he'll ever come back. And now Mother—she's going to marry this man and she won't care about me any more, and then I'll have no one. And what shall I do then?'

The last few words were cried out directly from her heart as she contemplated the bleakness of a life lived alone, without anyone to care for her. She thought of James in Paris, living with his Ginette, of her mother selling the antique shop and going off heaven knew where with her Brigadier, and the tears ran down her face and soaked into Troy's shirt. She sniffed and he felt in his pocket and brought out a clean handkerchief which he gave her.

'Listen,' he said, and she shifted her head slightly, to hear him better. 'Listen, I can't say anything about James; I don't know what the situation is there. But I can tell you for absolute certain that your mother isn't going to stop loving you just because she gets married again. In fact, you'll gain, because you'll have a stepfather who is kind and loving and already thinks quite a lot of you. But you have to face up to the fact that you're a big girl now, Rosalind, and you can't stay tied to your mother's apron strings any longer. She's trying to cut you free. Why don't you let her? What keeps you clinging on?'

Rosalind lifted her head. '*I'm* not clinging on,' she said indignantly. 'It's Mother—it always has been. She's driven me mad at times with her possessiveness. Always wanting me to ring her, to go down and see her. Oh, she never asks directly, but I know that's what she means. Little barbed remarks, you know, questions phrased so that you know they're really commands. She's always done it. And I've always gone along with it because—well, because I've known she was lonely and needed me. But I've always wished she'd stop it—always.'

'Are you sure?' he asked quietly. 'Are you sure that's what you've wished? Or were you really trying to keep her dependent on you?' He paused for a moment and then added, almost too quietly for her to hear, 'And isn't it possible that you've been doing just the same thing with your husband?'

There was a long silence. Then Rosalind began to cry again. The tears streamed from her eyes and down her cheeks. They soaked Troy's shirt, which had just begun to dry, and drenched his handkerchief. They dripped down her chin and ran down her neck and between her breasts. There didn't seem to be any way of stopping them. It was as if a dam had burst.

'Rosalind!' Troy held her close, rocking her in his arms. 'Rosalind, don't—you'll make yourself ill. Rosalind, Rosalind...'

Neither of them heard the door of the flat being unlocked. Neither of them heard the footsteps cross the hall. Neither of them heard the sitting room door open, nor saw the tall man who stood there, watching the little scene. And when James spoke at last, they both jumped as if they were guilty of the original sin itself and had just been caught in the Garden of Eden with their arms full of apples.

'It looks as if I've come at an inopportune moment.' His face was grim. 'Perhaps you'd like me to go away for an hour or so, until you've sorted out whatever seems to be bothering you.'

'*James!*' Rosalind gasped, and drew a long, shuddering breath.

Troy's arms fell away from her body. He started to get to his feet but James waved him back.

'No, don't get up on my account, please. I didn't intend to interrupt anything. You just carry on, while I do a bit of packing. Don't mind me, I just live here.'

'James, please listen—'

'Listen? Me?' His face was blandly enquiring but Rosalind knew that, behind the cool mask

194

he had assumed, there was a fierce rage burning. 'But I thought I had listened. Quite a lot actually, over the past few years. And you do seem to have a very efficient listener here now, so you won't be needing me any more, will you? So it's just as well I brought a large suitcase.'

He went out to the hall and came back with what was indeed a large, and obviously empty, suitcase. Rosalind watched in horror, then jumped up and ran to him, trying to pull the case from his hand. The tears had begun again but she ignored them, letting them run down her cheeks, almost accustomed to the feel of them by now.

'James, what are you doing? You're not—you didn't come home just to collect your things? You're not *leaving* me?' The fact that she'd almost persuaded herself over the past few weeks that this was just what he did intend to do, didn't lessen the shock now that it *was* happening. 'James, no! Please! We haven't even talked about it—we must talk about it. Oh, James, please, *please* let go of this wretched *case!*'

She pulled at his fingers but they were clamped tightly about the handle. She tugged at his arms, looked up into his face, but it was like stone. She looked desperately round at Troy but he was already on his feet and moving towards the door.

'Troy! You're not going? Please, you must

stay—'

'Oh yes, Troy,' James said in a hospitable voice, 'do stay. Why, you haven't even finished your coffee. You can't go yet, not just when things are getting interesting.'

'James, you've got it all wrong—'

'Have I?' His eyes moved to Rosalind's face and rested there for a moment, thoughtful as if someone had presented him with an intriguing puzzle. 'Perhaps you'd like to tell me just how I managed to do that?' His voice trembled suddenly. 'After all, it's past midnight and I've just walked into my own flat and found my wife in the arms of another man, obviously in the throes of some deep emotion. A scene that's easy to misunderstand, I know, but it seems to me that I've probably put the correct interpretation on it.'

He turned suddenly on Troy and the fury erupted on his face, naked and terrifying. For a moment, Rosalind was afraid that he meant to attack the other man, and she caught at his arms. He shook her off as if she were a fly.

'Perhaps *you'd* like to explain,' he snarled. 'Explain just what you're doing here with your arms around my wife, and why she's in such a state. Explain who the hell you think you are and just how you managed to worm your way into her affections. And I'd also like to know just how many times this has happened before, and what you intended to do about it? Or was it just a fling, a bit on the side while the old man was safely out of the way in France?'

'James, it wasn't like that at all—'

'Then tell me what it *was* like,' he said, and she saw him flinch at his own words. 'No.' He sat down slowly on a thin-legged, spindly chair that looked as if it would buckle under the weight of anyone over six stone. 'Don't. I don't think I could bear that.'

Rosalind stared at him. Suddenly, he looked very sad, very vulnerable.

She moved forwards, dropped on her knees beside him, took his hands in hers. 'James, Troy and I have been out to the theatre and to dinner,' she said. 'No more than that. We've had a nice evening and then he came back for coffee. *Just coffee.* And—well, I was upset about Mother and I told him about it and then I started to cry a bit and—'

'And he, naturally, took you in his arms to comfort you,' James said dully. 'And you let him. And there was a kiss or two, and one thing led to another and—'

'*No!*' It was so nearly what had happened on Troy's last visit here that she felt herself blush. 'No, James, that didn't happen. You must have seen for yourself—'

'But it would have happened. If I hadn't come in, it would have happened.' He looked her straight in the eye. 'Don't try to tell me it wouldn't have happened, Rosalind.'

Rosalind was silent. She couldn't deny that it might very easily have happened. She bit her lip and her eyes fell.

And then Troy, who had been silent, clearly embarrassed and wanting only to get away from this very domestic argument, stepped forwards. He sat down on the sofa, facing them both, and they looked at him.

'It wouldn't have happened like that,' he said firmly. 'Nothing else would have happened at all. Oh, I'm not saying I don't find your wife attractive, James—I'd be mad not to. She's a beautiful girl and if you don't mind my saying so, I think you ought to take better care of her. But I wouldn't have made any sort of a pass at her, tonight or any other night.'

He stopped, looking faintly embarrassed, and cleared his throat. 'You see, I have a wife of my own. We've been separated for a while—a few problems we couldn't seem to sort out together, and she went back to America, where her family lives, to think things out. And now she's coming back.'

There was a shadow of apology in his eyes as he glanced at Rosalind. 'I was going to tell you this evening but your problems rather overtook me. But I would never have jeopardised either your marriage or mine. I was simply what I wanted to be all along— your friend.'

Rosalind stared at him. 'But—but I thought—'

'You thought I wanted an affair—or maybe even something more.' He shrugged. 'Sorry—

but I never gave you any hint of that sort of intention, you know. It's always been friendship on my part, nothing more.' His eyes met hers and she knew he was thinking of that last visit here, when it might have turned into something more. She'd been relieved afterwards that it hadn't happened. Maybe he had been equally relieved. And now they were making a silent and mutual agreement to forget it had ever happened.

'I think you'd better go,' James said, and Troy nodded.

'I think so too. And no, I won't finish my coffee.' He glanced at the cup and his lips twitched. 'It's cold anyway.'

He rose to his feet and looked down at them both. His expression was cool, remote, as if already he were thinking of his own life, his own marriage. But there was a moment's warmth as his eyes rested on Rosalind's upturned face. And then he shifted his gaze to James.

'As I said,' he remarked evenly, 'you ought to take better care of her.' And then he walked out of the room and they heard the outer door open and close behind him.

There was a long silence.

'You—you aren't really leaving me, James, are you?' Rosalind asked in a small voice, and he turned his head towards her.

'I don't know. I don't know what I'm going to do.' There was pain in his face, but it surely

199

couldn't match the pain in her heart. 'The last few weeks—I've been torn apart, Rosalind. I've got to have time—time to sort things out. I've got to think.'

'Like Troy's wife,' she said. 'I didn't even know he was married, James.' A flame of anger began to burn somewhere deep inside. 'He ought to have told me he was married.'

'Why? If you were only friends, why should it matter?' James's eyes were sharp on her face. 'Maybe you didn't want it to stop at friendship. Maybe that's why you've been getting so upset lately—because you've fallen in love with another man and were afraid to tell me. Maybe it's nothing to do with you and me at all, nor with your mother. Maybe you were just using us to get rid of your own guilt!'

'No!' she cried, but even as she denied it she wondered somewhere deep in her mind if it could be true. 'No, it's not that at all. Troy's attractive and he's fun to be with and he *listens* to me, but I'm not in love with him. I'm in love with you, James—I always have been. That's why I want to be with you—why I didn't take Brent Woodford's job, why I didn't want you to go to work for IntInt and go to Paris. I want us to be *together*.'

'But why?' he burst out. 'Why do we have to be together all the time? Ros, I love you too but I don't want to live in your pocket. I want to be *me* and I want you to be *you*. Two individuals, with lives and minds and opinions of their own.

Two separate people who love and value and care for each other, but who can also function alone. Can't you see it that way? Doesn't it sound reasonable to you?'

Rosalind gazed at him. She heard his words, but the only ones that made sense to her were the ones that frightened her. She heard them again in her mind, tolling like bells. *Separate ... alone ...*

She shook her head. 'I don't see how you can love me and not want to be with me,' she whispered. 'I don't see how you can leave me and say you want to stay married to me. I love you and I want to be with you—to share my life with you. To share everything with you.'

James looked into her face, then stared down at the floor. He sighed heavily. 'And that, to me, just isn't love,' he said at last. 'It's possession, Rosalind. And you can't possess people. You can't own them. Mothers have to learn that about their children and children have to learn it about their mothers. Wives and husbands have to learn it about each other. But you've never learned it, Ros. You've never learned it about anyone. And that's why I can't stay with you.'

He stood up slowly, heavily, like an old man. Stricken into silence, she watched as he carried the empty suitcase into the bedroom. She heard him open doors and drawers, heard him close them again. A short time later he came out of the bedroom, with the case obviously now full and heavy, and he walked across the room.

Rosalind hadn't moved. She felt as if she had been frozen where she crouched. She looked up at him, and knew that her eyes must be huge in her pale, cold face. She saw him as if from a long, long way away, saw his face blur and sway and then bend close.

'Rosalind let me help you to bed. I'm going to stay till morning and then I'm going to ring your mother and ask her to come and look after you.' He lifted her to her feet and she went with him like a child, letting him undress her, slip her nightdress over her head, lay her in the bed and tuck the covers around her.

'I'm sorry about this, darling,' he said, sitting on the bed and taking her hand in his. 'I suppose this problem's been between us for a long time but as long as everything was going your way, you thought it was all right. I knew, though. I knew it wasn't right, our being so close. I just thought I could cope with it. And then when the Brent Woodford job came up, I realised what was happening to us and knew that sooner or later the crunch would come. Now it has, and we've got to face it. I'm sorry.'

Rosalind lay still, looking at him. Her lips were dry and she had to wet them with her tongue before she could speak. 'I still don't understand. What are you going to do? What do you want to do?'

'Just have a little time,' he said gently. 'Have

202

a little time and think about things. Think about what's happened between us and what I've said to you tonight. Try to see if you can't at least make an effort to understand.'

'And—Ginette?' she asked in a whisper.

'Ginette?' His brows came together in a frown. 'Rosalind, there's nothing between me and Ginette.'

Rosalind stared at him. She felt a sudden deep, cold contempt. After all that had passed between them, all his so-called honesty, he was still prepared to lie about his affair with Ginette? Even though Rosalind herself had heard her voice on the telephone that night, after she and James had made love and she'd really believed that everything could come right between them?

She heard the French girl's whisper again, heard her insinuating words. *''As she gone, James? Or is she still there?'*

Sickened, with a pain in her heart that was like a spear, thrust deeply in and slowly turning, she held her husband's eyes for a long, long moment. And then she turned away, unable to bear the sight of him any longer. 'Go away, James,' she said, her eyes closed, her voice dry and painful. 'Go back to Paris and think about whatever it is you need to think about. But don't come back here. Don't come back ever again, unless you're prepared to tell me the truth.'

Beside her, James made a sudden

movement, but Rosalind pulled herself deeper down into the bed and dragged the covers high over her head. She shrugged away his hand when he laid it on her shoulder. And although when he finally left the room she felt as if her whole life went with him, she did not stir again.

She lay quite still, sleepless, numb, until morning. And by then, James had gone.

CHAPTER TEN

'... so why don't you come down here for the weekend? Or longer, if you like. You must be lonely sometimes without James and it seems ages since we had you to ourselves.'

. Anna Camarthey's voice sounded warm and welcoming and Rosalind clutched the telephone to her as if it were a lifeline. The invitation was tempting and it sounded sincere—but how much did Anna know? How much had James confided in her?

'Have—have you heard much from James lately?' she asked, half dreading the answer.

'No, not for weeks.' Anna spoke cheerfully, and Rosalind wondered how her own mother would react if she hadn't heard from Rosalind for weeks. 'But no news is good news—I'd hear soon enough if anything were wrong. And I'm not the sort of mother who expects a blow-by-blow account of my children's lives.'

No, you're not, are you, Rosalind thought. And suddenly the idea of a few days in the big, untidy house with its haphazard furnishings and friendly warmth, seemed very attractive.

'I'll come,' she said quickly, before she could change her mind. 'I'll come on Friday, if that's all right. It does seem a long time since we saw you.'

'That's lovely. And don't go rushing back to London on Sunday evening if you don't have to. Stay on for a few days. It's beautiful down here now and we'd like to have you.'

'Yes, I'll try.' Rosalind thought quickly over her assignments. 'I might be able to take a couple of days' leave. I'll see what I can do.'

They rang off and she went back to her meal, feeling uplifted by the conversation. It might seem odd to be going to James's mother rather than her own, but so long as he hadn't told Anna anything, it didn't really matter, did it? And she certainly couldn't go to Sheila, with things as they were.

It was now almost three weeks since James had gone back to Paris, and during that time she'd had only brief notes from him. He had not telephoned, and neither had she. There was always the fear that if she telephoned the apartment, Ginette might answer, and Rosalind knew she couldn't have borne that. And if she rang the office she would have to speak to Lisa and, recalling her suspicions over the secretary, Rosalind felt awkward about that too. And in any case she didn't want to talk from her own office, and knew that James would find it equally inhibiting to speak in his.

Nor did she have any idea as to what they could say.

Rosalind had almost accepted now that James had left her for good. He was clearly in love with the little French girl and all his talk about Rosalind's possessiveness had been nothing more than an effort to clear his own conscience. If he could blame Rosalind for his own straying, if he could justify it by pointing his finger at her, then he could feel better about the pain he was inflicting.

The thought of what he was doing hurt her even more than the thought of his infidelity with Ginette. He was turning Rosalind's own love against her—the love that she had felt for him, the love she had believed he returned. He was using it as a scapegoat, turning it into some kind of monstrous snare, a prison from which he'd had to escape.

It was a worse betrayal than sleeping with another woman, Rosalind thought. He had sullied and spoiled something she had treasured, simply because he couldn't face his own shortcomings.

For a moment, she wondered if she were being wise in going to James's own home, to his own mother and father. But then reason reasserted itself. Why shouldn't she go? She had her own relationship with them that was nothing to do with James. She had her own friendships there. And she needed to see them. She needed their warmth, their undemanding friendliness, their easy affection that would let her come and go unquestioned.

And now that her mother was more interested in her Brigadier, she had no one else.

She thought for a moment of Troy. He had rung a day or two after James had left, cautious until he knew what had happened after he had left. He had been apologetic, telling her that he had never intended any compromising situation to arise. And Rosalind had believed him.

'I know,' she said honestly. 'It was all in my mind. I thought you were interested in more and I was scared about it, but I was half-inclined to go along with it. I'm not proud of myself, Troy, but I did feel so lonely and unhappy—and you were there, so sympathetic. I just got the wrong idea about us both.'

'Not your fault.' His voice was as warm as ever on the phone. 'I ought to have explained my own situation to you. And I'm more sorry than I can say if it caused difficulty between you and James.'

'Oh, he believed you. And our problems go deeper than that anyway.' She sighed. 'I don't know if we'll ever get them sorted out, Troy.'

'Well, I hope you do. I thought the first time I met you both, at your mother's, that you seemed ideally matched. Maybe a little time apart is all you need. It's helped me and Andrea, anyway.'

Rosalind made a wry face. Time apart was just what had caused the split between her and James in the first place, wasn't it? She couldn't see at all how it was going to help them now—especially if James was living with Ginette. If they weren't together, how could she prove to him how much she loved him?

'Well, I guess I'd better say goodbye,' Troy said at last. 'Not that it's going to be goodbye, is it, Rosalind? We shall still be in touch—you're going to go on with the cottage, aren't you? Andrea's mad about your designs and longing to meet you. And you'll be down from time to time to see your mother.'

'I suppose so. Yes, sometime. And of course I'm going to finish the cottage—that's business, anyway.' She couldn't admit to any longing to meet Troy's wife, who just would be called something like Andrea. 'I'm glad your wife likes my ideas,' she said politely.

Troy laughed. 'You'll like Andrea,' he declared. 'And now I must ring off. 'Bye, Rosalind—and thanks for everything.'

'Goodbye, Troy.' She put down the phone, shrugging ruefully. So that was that. She had a slight sense of deflation. It seemed that Troy had never felt more than a mild friendship for her. Oh, he'd been attracted, certainly, but he'd had no trouble in keeping that attraction well under control—probably because he was

208

obviously very much in love with his wife. And the few flirtatious or appreciative remarks he'd made about Rosalind had been no more than that—appreciation or mild flirtation. Anything more had been entirely in her own imagination.

Well, maybe it was just as well. She didn't need any more complications in her life, that was for sure. But with James presumably happy in Paris with Ginette, and her mother planning a new life with the Brigadier, it left Rosalind feeling very cold and lonely.

A weekend in Hampshire with the Camartheys might be just what she needed. She began to look forward to seeing them.

And they seemed equally pleased to see her. Anna was at the door as Rosalind stopped her car outside, her arms full of spring flowers from the garden. She came hastily to greet her, leaning over the clump of blossom and daffodils to deliver a kiss, and called over her shoulder to someone inside the house.

'She's here! Put the kettle on, will you? I'll just get rid of my boots—go in, Rosalind, everyone's waiting for you. I hope you don't mind—Laura brought the children to tea, they're dying to see you again. Haven't stopped talking about the lovely Christmas presents you brought them. Or the walk on Boxing Day—it was fun, wasn't it.'

She trod on the heel of one boot to hold it down while she pulled out her foot, then looked helplessly at the other. 'Oh, I always get caught like this—take these flowers, could you dear?'

Rosalind carried the flowers into the kitchen, where James's sister Laura was making tea. They greeted each other warmly and at the sound of their voices Laura's twins erupted from the sitting room where they'd been watching TV and began to caper about, talking at the tops of their voices and tugging at Rosalind's hands to gain her attention.

She kissed them and laughed at them and eventually, on the promise of a picnic in the woods next day, they went back to their TV programme, leaving the three women in the kitchen.

Rosalind watched them go a little wistfully. She and James had discussed having a family and decided to wait for five years before starting. Now she wondered if that had been wise. Would it have made a difference to their lives, to their marriage, if they had children like these to love and care for? She thought of the flat, so bare and white and empty. Suppose they had moved out of London—bought a cottage or a house like this one—and just let it grow around them? Would it have proved an anchor, somewhere they could have put down roots?

We've made a lot of mistakes, James and I, she thought sadly, and wished that she could have the chance to put them right.

She became aware that her mother-in-law was watching her, and smiled quickly and brightly. 'It's lovely to be here again. And the garden's looking beautiful. I don't know how you keep it so nice, with all you have to do.'

'Not so much, these days,' Anna responded. 'The house is always full when you're here, but most of the time Robert and I are on our own, so I have plenty of time. And I always make visitors help,' she added. 'For instance, you'll find your jobs listed on your bedroom door, and if you get through them before lunch I can soon find some more for you. And if—'

'Mum, stop it!' Laura exclaimed, and added to Rosalind, 'Don't let her bully you. She really will have you working if you're not careful—delightful little tasks like pulling up dandelions or collecting dead slugs from the beer-traps. Just say no.'

She got up from the table. 'And now I've got to go—see you tomorrow. Come on, you two,' she called to the twins, and they came scampering through.

Rosalind looked after them and then gave a little sigh and turned back. 'It must be nice for you to have Laura so close and be able to see her and the children whenever you like.'

'Yes, it is. I'm very lucky. But I think they're going to move away soon. Tim's applied for a post in Scotland.'

'In *Scotland*? But—you'll hardly see them.'

'Well, that's hardly the point, is it?' Anna

211

said with a smile of amusement. 'They have to lead their own life and I can hardly expect Tim to give up his career just so that I can have my grandchildren to tea. And it will be lovely to go there for holidays.'

'All the same ... all your children will be away then. You'll be so lonely.'

'I do have a husband,' Anna pointed out. 'And quite a busy life of my own. I shall miss Laura and the children at first, of course, but I don't think I'm going to be lonely.'

Rosalind shook her head. 'Well, I hope not. But I know my mother misses me.'

'Well, I expect she did when you first left home. Every mother does. But she's used to it now, surely? And she has her own life—her antique shop, her friends and so on.'

'Oh, I know, but it's not quite the same, is it? I'm all she's got, you see. And with Father dying so young—'

'Yes, it's been difficult for her,' Anna agreed. 'But she seems to me to have coped remarkably well. She has a very full life and obviously enjoys it. I shouldn't worry too much about her missing you, Rosalind.'

Rosalind looked at her in surprise. Anna had always seemed so sympathetic, so understanding. Yet now she spoke briskly, as if Sheila were no more than a child going off to school for the first time ... *'It's all right, she'll stop crying the moment you've gone, they always do.'* But Sheila wasn't a timid five-year-old. She was a mother, left alone at home. And she *does* miss me, Rosalind thought with a touch of indignation.

'I often wonder why she doesn't marry again,' Anna went on, blithely unaware of Rosalind's feelings. 'She's young enough, and attractive; she must have plenty of opportunities.'

Rosalind looked at her. She hadn't meant to come here and discuss her mother's life, but since the subject had arisen ... 'As a matter of fact, she *is* marrying again,' she said briefly. 'A man who's moved into the village quite recently—she's only known him five minutes. A retired Brigadier.' She spoke the words almost distastefully, as if she were confessing to some perversion of her mother's that the family had managed to keep secret until now.

A smile broke out over Anna's face. 'But that's wonderful! When did this happen? Have you met him? Is he nice? But he must be if Sheila's in love with him. And when is the wedding—'

'Oh, really!' Rosalind exclaimed, unable to stop herself from interrupting. 'You're as bad as everyone else. You think it's all romance and roses and you can't any of you see what a mistake Mother's making. *In love!* They're not teenagers, Anna. They're two grown people.'

'And can't grown people be in love?' Anna asked quietly. 'I'm still in love with Robert and he's in love with me.' She looked at Rosalind,

213

concern lining her face. 'Rosalind, what's wrong? I've known ever since I spoke to you on the phone that there was something.' She leaned across the table and touched Rosalind's hand. 'Is it you and James? You surely don't really believe that love stops when you grow older, do you?'

'No! At least—I don't know.' Rosalind shook her head violently. 'We were talking about Mother, not me. It's completely different.'

'Is it? Why's that?'

Rosalind floundered. 'Well, it *is*. She—she's my mother.'

'And therefore immune to normal human emotions?' Anna waited for a moment or two, then said gently, 'You really aren't happy about this marriage, are you, Rosalind? Why is that? Don't you like this Brigadier?'

'Oh, he's all right. Well, he's very nice really, I suppose.' Rosalind spoke grudgingly. 'I just feel—well, how does she know he's right for her? She's led such a sheltered life. I feel—well, I feel responsible in a way, I suppose.'

'But you're not responsible for your mother. And she's hardly had what I'd call a sheltered life—widowed with a young baby, making her own way in the world, running her own business, making lots of friends. I think she's very well equipped to make her own decisions. She's been doing it for a long time.'

'But she's depended on *me* so much! Oh, I

214

know there have been times when her possessiveness has made me want to scream, but I've always known she needed me. That's why I've always kept in close touch, writing and phoning two or three times a week, going to visit her. And now ... She stopped and rested her head on one hand, feeling the ache of tears in her throat.

'She doesn't seem to need you any more,' Anna said gently. 'Rosalind, are you really sure she ever did? Are you sure it wasn't you who wouldn't let go? Over-concern is sometimes a form of possessiveness, you know.'

Rosalind looked at her. 'Me? But—I left home years ago. I've built myself a career. I've got married—'

'And you've always kept in close touch—writing and phoning two or three times a week, going to visit her for weekends. Far more often than you and James come here—'

'Is that upsetting you?' Rosalind asked swiftly. 'Do you think we haven't come enough? But we try, we really do—and we have to have some life of our own. And with Mother—'

'No, of course I'm not upset. Don't add me to your burdens!' Anna reached for her hand, smiling at her. 'Rosalind, my dear, don't look so woebegone. I've always been happy to see you and James, and I've never felt you were neglecting me. Goodness me, don't you think I

215

have enough visits from my children? There are five of them—and when you add in the husbands and wives and grandchildren, it makes quite a crowd. The odd weekend when nobody at all comes to see us and Robert and I can actually do our own thing, is like an oasis of peace and quiet!'

Rosalind looked at her doubtfully. It had never struck her before that Anna and her husband might actually value their time together without any of their family around them. 'But this always seems such a family sort of house,' she said uncertainly.

'And so it is. But families grow up and go away. They make their own lives—create their own families and their own traditions. It's right and proper that they should do so. And parents can then make their own lives too. They usually did start off alone, you know, just the two of them,' she added gently. 'And must have been quite happy that way, don't you think?'

Rosalind gave her a wry glance. 'Yes, of course. But it's different for my mother. She only had me—'

'So she didn't have quite so much to get used to when you went away, did she?'

Again, Rosalind was brought up short and forced to see a different point of view. Yes, it must have been different for Anna, accustomed to a houseful, with five children flying the nest one by one … It must have

216

seemed very empty for a while. 'But you've got Robert,' she said. 'Mother was a widow. She didn't have anyone—'

'And now she's found someone.' Anna looked at her thoughtfully. 'So why can't you be glad for her, Rosalind? Why can't you feel happy that she'll no longer be so dependent on you? You say yourself that dependence has been a burden—why does it distress you so much to think of losing it?'

'It isn't that—' Rosalind began, but she broke off, because her heart was beginning to tell her that perhaps it was. 'Can't I just be concerned for her?' she broke out. 'Can't I just be anxious? She's my mother—I love her. I want her to be happy.'

'Of course you do. But only she can bring that about. It's not your responsibility.' Anna touched her hand again. 'I'm sure you would resent very deeply an interference by your mother—or anyone else—in your own marriage. And quite rightly so. So—'

'So why should I interfere in hers?' Rosalind finished for her, and sighed. 'I know. It's me that's wrong. But I can't help what I feel.'

'No, of course you can't. None of us can help what we feel.' Anna glanced at her. 'And ever since you arrived—I've had this feeling that there's something very wrong. Is it just your mother, Rosalind? Is that what's worrying you so much? Or is there something more?'

Rosalind sighed. The tears that were never

far away threatened her again. She felt the ache of them in her throat and all the pain of the past few months flooded her mind, overwhelming all other thoughts.

She looked at her mother-in-law and shook her head blindly, seeing the expression of concern change to one of real distress, reaching out both hands across the table and then drawing them back to cover her own face in a last attempt to mask feelings that could no longer be concealed.

'Rosalind! My *dear*—'

'Oh, Anna,' she said, weeping into her fingers, 'I'm *so* unhappy...'

*   *   *

Once again, Rosalind boarded the flight to Paris. Once again, she watched from the window as the plane taxied down the runway. Once again she saw the earth fall away beneath her and gazed down at the Channel, blue and sparkling today under a clear sky.

She'd had a long talk with her mother-in-law as they walked through the woods that evening and, although Anna had made no judgements, nor given any advice, Rosalind had known when they finished talking what she should do.

And Anna had agreed that it might be the best idea. 'You have to know what the situation really is,' she said. 'But—Rosalind, my dear—don't rush into anything. Make quite sure what it is you want before you do anything positive at all.'

'This is what I want,' Rosalind had said gravely, and turned for home.

She had spent a wakeful night, her mind racing with thoughts, many of them new and uncomfortable, but thoughts she was determined now to face. And very early in the morning, Anna had brought her a cup of tea and whispered that breakfast would be ready as soon as Rosalind came downstairs. And then she had set off for the airport, knowing that this was what she must do. For her own sake, and for James's sake. Neither of them could go on like this.

It was still early when the taxi drew up outside James's apartment. Rosalind got out and paid the driver, looking up with some apprehension at the building. Now that the moment had come, she found herself almost wishing that she were still at home, or in Anna's comfortable house. Or anywhere but here.

But that was the child in her, still shrinking away from life, afraid to face up to reality. Rosalind straightened her back and shoulders, lifting her chin. Hadn't she spent the whole night coming to terms with herself? Hadn't she made up her mind that if she wanted to be treated as an adult, she had to behave as one? With a firm step, she entered the building. OK, so she was still quaking inside—but nobody need know that.

The door to the apartment stood before her, closed, enigmatic. Was James in there? Was *Ginette* in there? She had a sudden sense of *déjà vu*, although the last time this scene was played it had been James coming through the door to find her in Troy's arms. She had a sudden flash of insight, knowing exactly how he must have felt. Was this how she too was going to feel a few moments from now?

She pressed the bell and waited.

For several moments, there was no sound from inside the apartment. She rang again, and a few seconds later heard padding footsteps. The door opened and James, tousled as if he'd only just got out of bed, peered out.

They stared at each other.

'*Ros...!*'

'Hello, James,' she said quietly. 'May I come in?'

'Yes—yes, of course.' He stepped back and Rosalind walked past him and into the big sunny room with its view of Paris's rooftops. 'Ros, I wasn't expecting you—'

'No. I know.' She glanced around the room. There didn't seem to be any sign of anyone else here. The bedroom door, leading from the living room, was ajar but she kept her eyes resolutely turned away. She hadn't come here to catch James out.

James came and stood in the middle of the room. His dark hair was ruffled, he wore only a pair of black silk pyjama trousers and his torso was already tanned. He looked slightly dazed, still warm from the bed, and Rosalind wanted nothing more than to go into his arms and then back to that bed with him ... But they had to sort things out first. They had to talk.

'Coffee?' he asked, and she nodded. As if relieved to have something to do, he disappeared into the kitchen and Rosalind sat down and waited. After a few moments he was back with two steaming bowls of coffee. He set them down on a low table and then dragged a cushion on to the floor and settled down on it. He looked at her, frowning slightly. 'Why have you come, Ros?'

'You haven't even kissed me yet,' she said, evading the question. But he didn't move and she felt ashamed. 'I came to talk.' She looked at him, at the dark, brooding face, the grave eyes. 'James—this isn't easy. Please help me.'

'What do you want me to do?'

She shrugged helplessly. 'I don't know. Make it easier for me, I suppose.'

James looked at her for a moment without speaking. Then he said, 'Rosalind, I don't know why you came here. I don't know what you want of me. I don't even know how you feel about me any more. How can I help you? How can I make it easier for you?'

She stared at him. 'You don't know what I want? *You don't know how I feel about you? But*—'

'How am I supposed to know?' he asked. 'You turned away from me, you refused to speak to me, you made it clear that I wasn't wanted. And since I left, you've rung me only once, wanting my sympathy because your mother's shaken herself free of you at last and decided to lead her own life. Well, I can't give you that sympathy. All I can say is—good luck to her! It's a pity she didn't do it years ago. You might have stopped thinking of yourself as the centre of the universe then.'

Rosalind gasped. She felt as if she had been struck. 'James, I didn't come here to—to—'

'To hear the truth?' he asked cruelly. 'No, I don't suppose you did. You've never wanted to hear the truth, have you? All you've wanted to do is swan through life as if it's an idyll—a sort of glossy, made-up fantasy that exists only in your own mind. Where people do what you want them to do—where everyone depends on you, because you're *Rosalind*, aren't you? Rosalind who dictates everything, who decides how the fantasy should be lived, who won't let anyone stray outside the magic circle because deep down she's just so insecure and possessive and downright jealous, she'd be afraid they'll never come back ... And maybe she's right, at that,' he finished sombrely.

Rosalind stared at him. His words hammered themselves into her brain. *Never come back ... never come back ... never come back...*

'Are you saying it's over, then?' she asked at last, her voice so dry and husky it was barely audible. 'Are you saying you want a divorce?'

'Isn't it what *you're* saying?' he asked bleakly. 'Isn't that the reason for this unannounced visit?'

Wildly, yet with a sense of utter helplessness, she shook her head. 'No! No, that's not why I came. I *don't* want a divorce—I never have done. I've never wanted to be away from you at all.'

She remembered her talks with Anna, the thoughts that had kept her awake throughout the night, and caught herself up. 'James, I know I've been too possessive. I've been insecure—frightened. That's partly why I've wanted us to be together—to work together. But there's another part too.'

She paused, trying to read his face, but his expression was shuttered, his dark eyes veiled. 'I love you, James,' she said shakily. 'I love you. I want to repair our marriage, not destroy it. I want to start again—to find a way that satisfies us both.'

She looked at him appealingly, lifting her hands palms upwards. 'Is there any chance?' she whispered. 'Is there any chance you'll come back to me?'

There was a long silence.

Then James sighed heavily. He looked at her hands and she thought for one wild, heart-fluttering moment, that he was about to take

223

them in his own.

But instead, he rose and walked over to the window, staring out at the panorama of the city spread below. 'What do you really want, Rosalind?' he asked at last, still turned away from her, still looking out over the city. 'Do you want everything to be as it was before? Do you want me to give up my job and come meekly back like a naughty puppy? Do you want me to sweep you into my arms, thanking you for condescending to notice me again, and take up just where we left off?'

He wheeled and faced her. 'Are you sure that what you really want isn't just to have me back under your thumb at Lords & Ladies?'

'*Under your thumb?*' She couldn't believe he was saying these things to her. What was happening? It was all going wrong—all her careful speeches, the truths she had faced during the night, the confessions she'd meant to make.

And then, suddenly, she realised that James was saying them for her. James was speaking all her own thoughts aloud. He was saying nothing she hadn't already told herself.

So why did she feel so disturbed? Just because he was reading her script?

She took a deep breath. 'James, please listen to me. I won't ask you to make it easy or tell me everything's all right again, as if I were a little girl. I know I've been behaving like one—and a spoilt one, at that. But I don't want to be a little

224

girl any longer. I want to grow up.' She gazed at him. 'I suppose I was asking you to make it easy for me to do that. But it's not easy, is it—for any of us?'

James said nothing. He watched her, then inclined his head slightly.

'James, I've been thinking a lot. And other people have helped me think—Troy and your mother, mostly. And my own mother too. But I've done most of it myself and—and I don't think I'm very good at it yet, so please bear with me if I still make a few mistakes.' She smiled tremulously but James's expression still didn't change. No, he wasn't going to make it easy for her, was he! And somehow that knowledge stiffened her resolve. She would show him that she *was* growing up!

'James, I realise I've been too possessive. With Mother—all the time I told myself she was clinging to me, it was really the other way about. And that's why I hated the idea of her marrying the Brigadier—because I was jealous.'

None of this was any easier than she had expected it to be, but she plunged on, determined now to say everything that was in her mind. 'And I've been too possessive with you, too,' she said bravely. 'I wanted to be with you all the time. I wanted us to work together, live together, do everything together. And I can see now it just can't work like that. Everyone needs to be an individual as well.

And you couldn't be, with me hanging around your neck all the time.'

James stirred and spoke. 'Rosalind, don't be too hard on yourself. I did enjoy working with you—'

'But not to the extent that you were prepared to put your career on ice for me. No, it's all right, James, I understand. I shouldn't ever have expected it. And I shouldn't have expected you to want me to do it, either. Neither of us ought to be standing still. But we ought to talk it out, decide what we really want out of life—and whether a career is really everything.'

James was watching her. 'Just what are you saying, Ros?'

She slipped from the chair and knelt beside him, putting her hands over his and gazing into his eyes. 'James, I want us to start again. Think out what we want and go for it—together, but as individuals. I don't want to possess you any more. I just want to love you—the way your mother loves your father. And I want to let Mother go, the way your mother's let all of you go, the way *you've* all let *her* go. I want her to be happy with—with Richard.'

James reached out and took her in his arms. He drew her close and she rested against the blessed warmth of his body, feeling his skin tremble beneath her touch. His breath was warm against her cheek and she lifted her face for his kiss. Slowly, he let her sink to the floor and lay close beside her, and she thought the kiss would never end and hoped that she was right.

Finally, he took his mouth from hers and whispered huskily, 'Ros, I've missed you so much.'

'Oh, James, have you? And I thought—' She felt tears come to her eyes and blinked them away, unable to say the words.

'You thought I was living with Ginette. Or at least having an affair with her.'

'I didn't know what to think. That day when I came before, I could see she wanted you and I thought you were attracted too. And then in the night, when she rang up—'

'You never gave me a chance to explain that,' he said soberly. 'And I was too damned stubborn to write to you. Let her believe it, if it's what she wants to believe, I told myself. My God, what a fool—I almost lost you through my own stupid, arrogant pride. And all over a flighty little French girl who would be better off as a china ornament on a shelf!'

'I thought she was a fairy from a Christmas tree,' Rosalind said, and felt him shake a little with laughter. 'But—if you weren't ha— having an affair with her—why did she telephone?'

'Just pure mischief,' he said. 'Worse than that—spite. She saw the way I was looking at you when you came into the office that morning. It was so sudden—so unexpected—it was like the sun suddenly blazing down through heavy clouds. I couldn't quite believe you were there.'

He paused, giving her a glance that was almost shy, and Rosalind remembered seeing the look on his face—a look that was suddenly illuminated with pleasure, delight, with love—and remembered also thinking that it had been directed at Ginette.

She felt shame wash over her in a great wave. It had been that moment that had convinced her that James was in love with the little French girl. She'd seen that look and hadn't even realised what it really meant. She had immediately, without stopping to reason, assumed the worst. 'Oh, James...' she said softly, and touched his cheek.

'I couldn't hide my feelings,' he went on. 'They must have been plain on my face, for everyone to see. Ginette certainly saw. And she was jealous. Not that she had any reason to be jealous, but simply because she likes to be the centre of attention, always. She's the spoilt brat to end all spoilt brats and, like a spoilt child, when she doesn't get what she wants she stamps her feet and screams. Or, in this case, tried to cause trouble by making indiscreet telephone calls in the middle of the night. And she succeeded too. Ros, how could we do it? How could we let that silly bit of nonsense come between us?'

'It wasn't just that,' Rosalind said slowly.

'James, there's been something wrong with our marriage for a long time. We've been drifting apart, so slowly we didn't even notice it.' She looked at him. 'Was it just my possessiveness? Or was there something more?'

He held her close without speaking for a long time, then he said, 'I think we have to look and see why you felt that way, Ros. Why you were so insecure. We have to know what you were really feeling. Do you know? D'you think you can tell me?'

She frowned a little. 'I don't know. All I ever wanted was to make you happy. And I thought I was. But then—I started to feel lonely, James. It was as if something was missing. And I think I held on to you all the more tightly, to try to fill the gap.' She looked at him and added quickly, 'I don't mean you weren't enough for me. But—'

'But I can't be enough for you,' he said. 'Nobody can be enough, all by themselves. We all need other things in our lives—work, home, a family . . . Is that what you're missing, Ros? Is it a family you want? A baby?'

'Perhaps. We always said we would, didn't we? But even before that . . .' She suddenly began to feel on surer ground, as if some deep, half-recognised mystery were beginning to become clear. 'Even before that, you need a home. And our flat in London isn't.' She hesitated before continuing, then went on bravely, 'The cottage I've been decorating for

229

Troy Ballard—there really wasn't anything between us, James, though there could have been—it's so much more a home than our flat could ever be. I could imagine a family there. I can't imagine one in the flat. Can you?'

James laughed a little. 'No, indeed. All that white, just asking to be scribbled on! So what are you saying, Ros?'

'I'm not quite sure,' she said slowly. 'But I think I'm saying that our entire way of life is wrong. We thought it was right because it seemed to be the way young designers like us ought to live. But it isn't right—not for us.'

He drew away slightly, so that his eyes could meet hers. His fingers stroked her cheek. 'So what do you think *is* right?'

Rosalind paused, choosing her words carefully. She was aware that this was a vital moment in their story. If it went wrong now— they might never be able to put it right. If James's ideas were too opposed, his needs too different...

Suddenly, she wasn't sure any more that she knew what his needs were. She wasn't sure that she knew him. 'James, I don't think I want to live in London any more. I'd like to live somewhere in the country. Hampshire, perhaps, or Sussex, or the Cotswolds—but not too near either of our families. I want us to find our own way. And,' she glanced at him timidly, almost shyly, 'yes, I'd like us to think about starting a family.'

'A family,' he said, almost wonderingly.

She nodded, her face suddenly on fire with excitement. 'Yes. James, I was at your mother's yesterday and I looked around and suddenly I knew that *this* was what I wanted. A *home*. Not a showplace, perfectly furnished and decorated but a real, untidy, family home with bits and pieces we've collected because we like them, not because they match each other, and children's toys on the floor and pets and—'

'Hang on!' he protested. 'What about your job? Your career?'

'Well, I'd have to give up Lords & Ladies of course,' she admitted. 'But I thought—why not do as Mother did? Run a small business—an antique shop perhaps, or maybe interior design just locally. Or design fabrics, or—oh, there'd be *something*, James. I wouldn't have to vegetate.'

'No, you wouldn't. I can't imagine you ever vegetating.' He pulled her close again and murmured into her hair, so that the words were almost lost, 'What would you say to a *chateau* in France?'

Rosalind lay quite still. She tried to decide whether she had actually heard him or not. Then she drew back and stared at him. '*What* did you say? A *chateau* in France?'

'That's right. You know the one I've been working on—well, the owner's decided to sell after all. And it's a delightful place—just a pleasant country house really, with lots of

231

space for nurseries and children's toys and a business too. Not exactly Hampshire or the Cotswolds, of course, but within easy distance from Paris. And—'

'You're suggesting we buy it? But—'

'I'm not really suggesting, no. Just putting it out as a thought. With prices the way they are at home and here, if we sold the London flat we could just about afford it. And IntInt have offered me a permanent post in charge of the French end of the business.'

She felt the muscles of his face twitch against hers. 'I was trying to decide whether to mention it or not. I didn't think you'd want to move so far away from your mother. But if she's getting married again...'

He paused, and then said in a very low tone, 'I didn't even know whether you'd want to come and live in France with me. Or live with me anywhere at all, come to that.'

'James...' Rosalind stared at him. 'Oh James, how could you ever doubt it? Of course I want to be with you! It's all I've ever wanted...' She buried her face against his chest, feeling the tears flow from her eyes. 'James, you don't honestly mean you thought—you thought I didn't love you?'

'I didn't know what to think,' he said. 'You've been so unhappy just lately. As if you didn't know what it was you wanted. All the worry over your mother—and then this Ballard appearing on the scene. Don't think I

232

couldn't see the attraction—that smooth sort of type, all gloss and charm, why, you'd be bound to be attracted. I mean, what have I got to offer when a chap like that sets out to—well, you know. And being miles away during the week, knowing you were there on your own—well, I couldn't help imagining all sorts of things.' He glanced at her apologetically. 'It's not that I don't trust you, Ros, don't think that. But—'

'I know,' she said quickly, thinking guiltily of the two evenings she had spent out with Troy, the woodland walks, the pub lunches. 'And I can't honestly say that I wasn't attracted—just a bit. But it was just because I was lonely, James, there was nothing more in it than that. And it never went anywhere.'

They were both silent for a few moments.

Rosalind thought over her own words. *Just because I was lonely*. She had had the same thoughts about James. She had imagined him in Paris, lonely without her and turning in his loneliness to someone else—to Lisa, to Ginette. To almost any woman he came in contact with. 'Oh, James,' she said shakily, 'what have we been doing to each other?'

He gathered her close against him and she felt the beat of his heart against her breast. He bent his head and laid his lips on hers, then moved his mouth slowly along the curve of her cheek. 'I think we just lost our way for a while,' he said quietly. 'I think we forgot what loving

233

and marriage was all about. We forgot everything but our work, so when you turned down that offer from Brent Woodford, I was angry because you'd passed up the opportunity to move up the ladder, and moreover you'd done it without consulting me—and you were upset because you saw moving away as a blow to our relationship, and thought my insistence on it showed that we were already drifting apart.' He stopped and lifted his head a little so that he could look into her eyes. 'Does that seem a fair assessment to you?'

'Yes, it does. And then when you took the job in Paris—I was devastated. I thought you just wanted to get away. As if I were stifling you. You didn't want to work with me any more.'

'But I did,' he said. 'I hoped a chance would come up for you to join me. I said so.'

'And I thought you were being patronising.' She sighed. 'We've been talking different languages, haven't we.'

'Perhaps men and women always do,' he observed. 'And the best thing we can do is start learning each other's as fast as we can!'

'Oh, James,' she said. 'I'm sorry for my suspicions. I'm sorry if I've been possessive and jealous. You were right about me and Mother. I do think she clung on to me more than she should have—but I didn't really discourage her, did I? I liked the feeling that she couldn't do without me—until *I* began to feel stifled too.'

'I'm sorry too,' he said. 'I should have realised how lonely you would be. I could have done more about that—but I suppose I was angry.'

'We've both been rather silly, haven't we,' she whispered, and he smiled and shook his head.

'Now, whenever have you heard a man admit to being *silly*? We've been human, Ros, that's all. And now,' he moved his body against hers and she felt a sudden sharp thrill, 'I think it's time we proved just how human we can be.'

'James...' she whispered, and then said no more as his mouth found hers again, hard with urgent passion. Her response leapt within her like a flame as she wound her arms about his neck and pressed herself against him, lost to everything but the joy of knowing that they were back in tune, the discord of the past months now safely behind them as they faced the future once more together. 'James, I love you...'

'And I love you too,' he murmured against her neck. 'Oh Ros, my darling, darling Ros, I love you so much ... When I woke up that morning and you were gone—when I thought I'd lost you—Ros, I thought I was going to lose my mind. You're all that matters to me, you know that? There's nothing—nobody, nobody—in this whole world that matters to me as much as you do.'

She heard his words through a haze of emotion, where joy was mixed with pain, and pain with learning. I should have known, she thought. All the time I was suffering and thinking only of my own unhappiness, I should have known he was suffering too. We should both have known.

'I'm all yours,' she told him softly. 'There isn't anyone else in the world that matters to me, either, as much as you do.'

'Not even—' he began, and she looked at him and caught the wicked glint in his eye.

'Not even—*anyone*,' she said, with a little laugh. 'It doesn't matter who they are, they'll have to manage without us from now on. They'll have to plan their own lives.' She touched his lips with hers. 'And we,' she murmured, 'will have a lovely time planning the rest of our lives. In a French *chateau*, with children leaving their toys everywhere and Mum slaving away in some little back room while Dad earns the real money in the city. Is that what you had in mind?'

But James shook his head. 'No, it isn't, quite. Just at first, perhaps, but then ... I thought we might work together again, Rosalind. In this business you're going to set up. You see, we do work very well together, we make a good team. And in our own business we could hit the heights together, with no competition between us, no sense of one holding the other back or going on alone. Two individuals, each bringing our own skills and talents to the job. And there's another advantage too.' He looked down at her and grinned a little self-consciously. 'That way, I'd get to help look after the kids as well!'

Rosalind stared at him, then flung back her head and laughed. Her laughter rang through the slowly awakening Paris morning. And it only stopped when James laid his lips on her arched neck and drew them down to her throat in a long, tender kiss.

Her laughter died away. She felt his hand cup the back of her head, lifting her towards him.

She let her lips part to meet his, and took his hand and laid it on her breast. 'Let's go to bed, James,' she whispered, and he swept her up into his arms and carried her through the bedroom. Where Ginette was not, nor had ever been.

Where there were only the two of them, herself and James, close and loving, sealing their word on this new life they had planned together.